# DOWN A DARK ROAD

# Down A Dark Road

## A Collection of Short Horror Stories

TARYN WOMACK

Taryn Womack

I want to thank my best friends and my family for rooting for me from the very beginning and pushing me to be my best.

# CONTENTS

# JOY

This is the only time I feel true joy. I have been raised as any girl could ever wish. My parents spoiled me and gave me anything I could ever want. In return, I had to be the best. I got the best grades in school, I took on as many sports as I could fit into my schedule, I became class president, and I volunteered; I became the poster child of "the golden girl." My parents were always so proud of me, and when I made them proud, they gave me anything I asked for.

But it seemed that no matter how much I accomplished or how many hobbies I picked up, I could never gain any joy from it. I never felt any emotion, honestly. Maybe anger or frustration, but I'm not quite sure. I've certainly never felt happy or excited. I've had to fake all the smiles and laughs in my life. For the longest time, I had concerned my parents because they simply thought I was an unhappy child, but it wasn't that I wasn't happy or sad; I was just there, existing. I learned very quickly that I disliked it when people would ask me how I was feeling because I never knew how to respond. I couldn't just say I'm not feeling anything because people would think I'm weird, and I don't want that. So, I learned how to fake my emotions; I learned when it was appropriate to be happy or sad. I taught myself to cry on demand because my cousin had pointed out that she had never seen me cry, not even at funerals. I've gotten very good at faking it; I believe I might have a promising career as an actress in the future.

It's quite unfortunate, really, not being able to feel anything. I believe I miss out on a lot of things: the excitement of getting a new puppy, the pain of losing someone, or being able to love someone. Love has always been described to me, and my family always tells me how much they love me. I tell them I love them too, so I don't hurt their feelings, but I've never felt like that, like love. I've never loved a pet or a friend. I have found them to be a nuisance in my life, taking more of my time than necessary, but they are needed to portray a sense of normalcy, right?

It's quite funny; I thought I would spend the rest of my life without any feeling, without any emotion towards someone or something. I thought I'd marry someone I didn't care about and force myself to have children I'd never feel motherly towards. I wasn't looking forward to any of it. But I had found something that brought out this strange desire I couldn't place. I was watching an old slasher movie with my mother a few months ago. It was the first time I'd seen a scary movie; they thought I was too young for that type of thing. But they let me watch it, and for the first time, I believe I felt an emotion. It wasn't fear, and I don't think it was adrenaline from the suspense. It was like I was drawn to it; the movie had captured my interest so rapturously; I didn't even know how to react.

Since then, I have been watching as many scary movies as I could. I would watch them when my parents were gone or when I was supposed to be studying so they wouldn't get upset. I watch many different types: slashers, paranormal, psychological, and so on. I had found that I got the feeling when the protagonists were stuck in their situation and – what I'm guessing most people would describe as dread – loomed over the atmosphere. The antagonist had control over the protagonist; they held their lives in their hands. It got me thinking about how that translates into real life, so I went on a bit of a research spiral, looking up serial killers and murder mysteries. Do you know how many serial killers there have been just within the last 30 years? Almost 2000. Can you believe it?

They all had such fascinating ways of killing. I found myself drawn more to two types of serial killers: those who tortured their victims before killing them and those who had distinct signatures. Charles Albright removed his victims' eyeballs. Jack the Ripper was an over-killer; he brutalized his victims so bad it was the only thing that connected them. The Monster of Florence would mutilate the victims' genitals and then take a body part or trinket as a souvenir. Then you have the famous ones, like Ted Bundy, Jeffery Dahmer, Richard Ramirez, and my personal favorite, H.H. Holmes.

Now he was a creative man. He is the guideline for a

perfect serial killer. He built a whole hotel just to trap people and torture them to death. He was a smart man, too; he found many ways of getting the life savings of his victims before killing them: he seduced them, he forced his employees to put him as their beneficiary, and of course, he simply stole it. He even sold some of his victims' bodies to the universities. He only confessed to 27 murders, but the suspected count is actually all the way in the 200s. Can you believe it? He killed over 200 people and only went down for 27, extraordinary.

Learning about these men and women has really set a fire in me, learning about all the different ways people were tortured and killed, brutalized, and mutilated. Knowing that they spent their last moments knowing they were going to die and there was absolutely nothing they could do about it. I watched a few documentaries, and listening to how some of these killers felt when they would kill is almost exciting. I get excited listening to them, the way they talk about how their victims would beg or cry or scream, and they got to revel in the power they held over them. They were a god at that moment, holding life and death at their fingertips. Can you imagine how that feels? I wanted to know how that feels.

I didn't start with animals; that's too obvious. That is how all the stories start: "They killed their neighbor's cat or the rabbits in the woods," I didn't want to make anyone suspicious. Besides, I wouldn't get the satisfaction from an animal; they can't speak, and sure, they can scream and whine, but it's not the same. I had to plan to the most minute detail. Where would I go, who should I bring first, and how should I do it? All these questions ran through my head, so I had to plan it out in my journal. After it was all figured out, it was almost too easy.

I figured the best way to lure someone in was to go after someone who saw themselves as a predator. I believed it was the easiest way, and I figured I would gain ample satisfaction from watching the roles switch: predator to prey. It did, by the way. Watching the glow and hunger drain from his eyes until all that was left was hopelessness; it was exhilarating. With every cut of his flesh and snap of his bone, I felt that fire and those emotions well up, and I laughed, genuinely laughed, for the first time in my life. I became addicted; I needed to feel it again. But I had to be smart; I couldn't let anyone think it was me, I couldn't link any of my victims, and I had to be very clean.

I found this place while hiking one day. It was obviously abandoned, and so far from the rest of town, no one would know a thing. I would dig a nice deep hole beforehand, so I didn't have to waste time after; my parents believe I'm in the gardening club. Then, I tell the man to meet me at the hiking trail and lead him to my little playhouse. These men are so stupid that they think they're going to get exactly what they want: a young, naïve little girl all to themselves to violate. I know you can picture the looks on their faces when I drug them just enough to manhandle, tie them to a chair, and have my way with them. Then when I'm all done, I carry them to the hole outside, throw the bloody clothes in with them, and cover them up. It's a rush of excitement and joy.

"And I'm sure you're wondering why I'm telling you all this. You just want me to kill you and get it over with. But I know you're wondering why. Why are you doing this? Why me? That's what they always ask. So, I wanted to tell you, so you understand." There wasn't much emotion left on his mutilated face. There was more blood than skin; red flowed from his mouth where his teeth used to be. It was a beautiful sight, watching every finger try to move in their broken state, chest shallowly rising as blood filled his lungs, he was dying, and he knew it. He can't get away; he can only pray that his afterlife is kind to him. That light in his eyes when we first met today shone a bright blue as they looked over my teenage body. They became even wilder the closer we got to the playhouse, away from everyone. Now, those eyes were so swollen he won't even be able to see the final blow; tragic, really.

He had stopped begging not long ago, and it was getting boring; the feeling was starting to fade. I guess it's time to finish it. "I want to thank you for letting me feel; I'm very grateful for your sacrifice." A giggle bubbled out of me, and an odd thrill ran down my spine. There were only a few times I had genuinely laughed, and each time felt even better. The man, whose name I didn't care to remember, didn't even struggle or cry out before I smashed the hammer into his temple. There was only a grunt before he went silent forever. I took a breath and let the feeling resonate. The buzzing will last for the next hour or so; I need to hurry and quickly clean up so I can enjoy it.

I untied the man from the chair and dragged him the short way to the door. It's moments like these that I can appreciate my effort in training hard for sports; otherwise, I would not have the strength to do this. The hole was already dug, five feet down and thick enough for the body. I threw him in and marveled at the sound of his body crashing into the dirt. I took the time to clean myself, removed the gloves and cap on my head, took off my outer layers of clothing and shoes, and threw it all into the hole. I changed into my "gardening" clothes and got to work covering him up.

After six times, the cleanup has gotten easier. I don't have to worry about the inside because no one will ever go in there. I was able to start walking home, not even 45 minutes later. It was a lovely night; the sun had just set completely, and the coming summer had warmed the air. With the buzzing through my veins, I could actually enjoy the feeling of it on my skin. The walk took thirty minutes, and I called my parents when I arrived. "I'm home!" I entered my house and slipped off my shoes. When my mother rounded the corner, I put on a smile and greeted her as expected.

"Hey, my little Joy. How was your day?" She hugged me tightly, and I returned it with a matching strength.

"Joy, dinner's almost ready!" My father called from the kitchen.

"My day went well, nothing special," I replied with a familial tone and continued my evening routine. I'll have to start looking for my next one; I don't like how fast the feeling goes away.

# DREAM HOUSE

The new house was a dream. The tall Victorian stood on an acre of land with beautiful trees fencing the border; they had lovely white flowers that blew in the wind, making the scene look like a fantasy. I had been saving for years to be able to put a down payment on my first house, and to be able to find one like this in my budget was unreal.

The house itself was one I had always pictured myself owning. It was your stereotypical Victorian with a tall turret roof on the right side and a long, wrap-around porch along the left side. It was painted blue to match the sky, with white trimming on the edges and the windows. The interior was made of dark brown wood and ivory walls. The wooden staircase wound up from the main hallway to the second floor, holding four rooms. The master was my favorite: a large bedroom that already came with a queen bed, hand-crafted with four tall posts. The attached bathroom had a clawfoot tub! I've always wanted one. Everything about the house was a mixture of old and new and perfect. The moment I saw the pictures online I fell in love; I knew this was my house, and for the price, I couldn't turn it down.

The first day I stepped into the house, I felt like I stepped into my dream. I felt a continuous buzz of excitement and wanted to run around the house and explore like a child at a new playground. "You sure you're not gonna be lonely in this big house by yourself?" My dad asked as he helped carry in my boxes of stuff.

I laughed and sat on the couch that came with the house; all the furniture came with the house, which made the deal even sweeter. "I'll be just fine, Dad. Besides, I'm sure Kayla and Brandon will be over enough to never feel alone," I chuckled. My best friend Kayla and my boyfriend Brandon had already made it clear that they would be here all the time.

"I know, it's just," he paused and looked around the living room, "don't you think this place is a little off?" He scratched the back of his neck like he normally does when he's nervous. I guess that's kind of understandable. The main reason the house was so cheap was because of the... not so great history of it. "I'm just saying, Lizzie, I think you should have Kayla or Brandon move in or something, just so you're not by yourself."

I sighed and stood up, "I get you're worried, but Kayla has her own place, and Brandon and I aren't ready for that just yet. I assure you I'm going to be fine." I pulled him into a hug. "All the stuff that happened is in the past. In fact, I feel great in this house; I feel at home."

He sighed and pulled back to look at me. "I just want you safe, Pumpkin."

"I know, Dad, and I am." He nodded, and we finished getting all my stuff out of the mover's van.

Around noon, Kayla showed up, "Who's ready to party!" She shouted as she came in, but it turned into silent awe as she looked around the house. "Wow, this place is beautiful." She joined my dad and me in the kitchen and placed a bottle of wine on the island. "How did you get a place the this?"

"I have a good agent," I chuckled. This was also true; she found this house quickly and was very honest about everything, which I appreciated because not many would've been.

An hour later, the door opened again. "Hey, Beauti-ful." Brandon came in and placed a pizza on the counter before kissing my forehead.

The rest of the day went by as you may expect, we tried to get unpacked but ended up getting a little wine drunk and lounging on the couch. We did get some stuff unpacked, though, so I didn't have to do too much by myself tomorrow. Dad had left at around 5 to pick up Mom from work. He kissed me on the head goodbye and told me to stay safe.

"Why was your dad so freaked?" Kayla asked. Dad had been anxious the whole time he was here, it would've been hard to miss.

I sighed, "He's a little freaked over the history of this place." They both quirked an eyebrow at the statement. "Well, I got this place for cheap because it doesn't have the best history." I got up and grabbed the folder of documents my real estate agent gave me from my new office space and plopped it on the table. "The place was built back in the 1800s; the owner was this rich guy who built the house for his wife and two daughters. They seemed to be a pretty normal family to the public, but some secrets came out after they died." I opened the folder and pulled out the first document, a newspaper clipping from 1846. "He was a nasty dude. He butchered his wife and kids, then hung himself in the attic." They both looked at the clipping, and I could feel Kayla shiver. "From the statements the police got, he was super controlling. The only time the rest of the family was seen outside the house was with him; other than that, they never left. The police found chains and large blood stains in the basement."

"And you bought a murderer's home?" Kayla asked, astonished.

I huffed a laugh and elbowed her a little. "That was over 100 years ago. Some things happened after, though." I pulled the next few out. "Once the place was cleaned up and turned around, it was bought by this older couple who passed away peacefully in the bedroom, then in 1923, shit got weird again."

"Oh, goody." Brandon joked and took a sip of his wine.

I pulled out a couple more papers. "The house turned into this mental home of sorts. It was bought by Ingrid and Jameson Poole to be a home for lost girls. Basically, a home for girls that were mentally ill, but their families didn't want them to go into psych wards. Anyway, the 'business' stayed open for about ten years. A lot of girls went in, but very few ever came out. But that was kind of expected at the time because they were sick. Plus, it's not like anyone was going to question the people taking care of their burdens." I scoffed; the first time my agent told me the story, it made me sick.

"Well, one family, the Allenders, started asking questions after their 16-year-old daughter died. She had been sent there because she attempted suicide, but there weren't any other records. Her parents loved her and didn't want her in a bad place, so they sent her here, expecting her to get help and be out in a few months.

"According to the articles, they had said they got some weird letters from their daughter, saying things like how she was scared of the place, that the nurses were mean, and that girls went missing at night. About two months after she got there, she died. The Pooles said she killed herself; she got into the medicine cabinet and took what she could. But her parents didn't want to believe that, especially with the letters, right? So, they called for an in-depth autopsy and found she was poisoned with arsenic.

"Because of this, the police got involved and found some really fucked up shit. The couple had been doing some horrible things to those girls. They tied them to the beds, starved them, the husband raped them, they would lock them in the basement for days until they starved to death or went even more insane, then they killed them but made it look like they did it to themselves." I shook my head. "They were arrested and sentenced to death in 1934."

"That's so horrible," Kayla whispered, and Brandon nodded in agreement.

"Yeah, I almost got sick listening to the story from Ellis." I heard Kayla whisper, "What the fuck" under her breath. "After that, the house was empty until 1962 when a group of friends bought it. They were all into satanic shit and used the house as their home base. They used the basement for their rituals and sacrifices. As far as I know, they didn't do anything to humans, but still, it's pretty creepy. They left in '76; the house had two other owners who seemed pretty normal since then. The last owners died in the house about three years ago, and they didn't have any other family, so the house has just been sitting with all their stuff."

"So, this is a dead person's couch?" Kayla asked with a disgusted voice.

"They didn't die on the couch, dork." I closed the folder back up and sat back. "I know I'm the weirdo for buying such an insane house, but I don't feel anything wrong with it, you know? It doesn't feel bad."

"If you say, dude, I couldn't see myself ever living here," Kayla said and got up. "I'm gonna head home; I got work tomorrow. Later guys!" She shouted as she shut the front door.

"What do you think of all this? You've been quiet." I leaned against Brandon, and he wrapped his arm around my shoulder.

"It's definitely weird. If it were me, I would've laughed as soon as she explained that a murderer lived here. But, I trust your judgment, and I know this is someplace you've been dreaming about, so I'm here to support you." He kissed my head and smiled.

"Thank you." I gave him a quick kiss and got up. "Do you want to stay tonight? We could break in the new place." He chuckled as I leaned to kiss him again.

"As much as I would love to, I have to get home; I have an early morning tomorrow." He kissed me once more and stood up. "But I think I can help break in the place next weekend." We both laughed, and he hugged me tightly. We said our goodbyes, and I was alone for the first time in my new house.

The night was quiet, the only noises coming from the rogue car driving down the street, the bats hunting for food, and the little creaks from the house settling. All normal sounds, in fact, some would say it was the perfect environment to fall asleep in. But I couldn't get my brain to fall asleep; admittedly, I felt like I was on high alert. Every sound felt like it was right next to my head; I felt like every creak was a pair of footsteps walking to my door. Maybe it was just being in a brand-new place alone for the first time in my life. My brain wasn't used to it, and it thought I was in danger.

I sighed, I felt wide awake so I decided to use the time wisely. I got out of bed and headed downstairs to work on unpacking a few more boxes. I couldn't stand how quiet it was, so I played music through my little speaker, only loud enough for the room to hear; I didn't want to disturb the neighbors.

It was about three in the morning; I had finished putting away everything in the living room and the kitchen. I looked around, quite satisfied with my work. It's amazing what you can get done without any distractions. I still didn't feel tired. I was going to die tomorrow from exhaustion. Hopefully, I could get a nap in at least.

I headed down the hallway to the back room, which held the laundry area and the door to the basement. When I first toured the house, the number of boxes stored down there was shocking. As I said, the last owners had left everything here, so all their stuff got piled into boxes. I figured it would be a good idea to look through it; maybe I could sell some of it.

The basement was about ten degrees colder than it was upstairs. It was a large concrete room with wooden pillars and rafters holding it up. The boxes lined the farthest wall, and there were a few more pieces of furniture: a large curio cabinet, some dark wood side tables, and a couple of dressers made of similar wood, all expensive looking. A few trash bags, probably clothes and towels, were piled against the wall closest to the stairs. I walked to those; *I can donate these once I go through them.* I started picking them up and froze once I saw the floor.

There was a dark mark on the floor against the wall. It was small but noticeable, I leaned down to get a closer look, and I almost felt the urge to touch it to see if it was wet. But why would there be a wet spot? It was under all those bags, and it's completely dry down here. Still, my brain wanted to know, so I reached my hand out and touched the dark spot. I let out a breath I didn't realize I was holding when my fingers returned dry. It must be an old stain; it brought my mind back to the stories Ellis told me. Was this a stain from the family, from one of those poor girls? I shivered thinking about it.

A loud creak brought me from my thoughts. I whirled around to look at the dimly lit room. *Great, now I'm freaked out, and the settling noises are scaring me.* I sighed and got up from my spot. "Calm down, Liz, you're fine." I walked over to the stacks of boxes; this would take a while to go through. I went to grab one but froze at the noise above me. It wasn't the usual creaks that had been going on all night; they weren't creaks at all. They were heavy thuds, repeating themselves as they moved. They started right above me and moved back to where the door would be, *thud thud thud thud*, like the footsteps of a big man. No, they couldn't be footsteps; that would be crazy. Unless someone broke in. Right above me would be the living room; it is possible someone could've broken in. I didn't like that the idea of someone breaking in scared me less than my first thought.

I listened carefully, the thuds continued, and they were getting closer to the basement door. I felt my heart beat faster, waiting for the intruder to come down the stairs. I looked around the room for something to defend myself with, but the best I could probably do was throw a box at him. I got ready, listening, *thud thud*, louder and closer.

Then as they were right at the top of the stairs, they stopped. My ears strained, trying to find any noise, any indication that he was coming down the stairs. But it was silent, completely silent, no creaks and groans from the house, no sign of movement of any kind, not even my own breathing as I held it.

After what felt like forever, but was probably only a minute, I walked back to the stairs and looked up at the open door. The light illuminated the room and the top few stairs. Still, no other sound came from the floor above. I took a deep breath and decided to brave it. I took one stair at a time, each one giving a harsh creak as the old boards heaved under my weight. I got to the top of the stairs and peeked my head out of the doorway. There wasn't anyone up there. Nothing indicated anyone had been there.

I kept my pace slow as I checked the side door, it was shut, and when I checked the knob, it was still locked. I walked to the front of the house, but still, nothing looked touched or moved. The door was closed, and all the locks were still in place.

*I can't believe this; this isn't real, right?* I looked around the living room, hoping something would prove another person was there. If that wasn't the case, I must've just been really tired, but I didn't realize it. *I'm hearing things, that's all. That has to be the answer; I was hearing things in the old house because I was super tired.* I sighed and rubbed my eyes; *maybe I should try going to bed. The boxes can wait until the morning.*

Retelling the first event to Kayla and Brandon felt like an elephant was moved off my chest. It had been six months since that first day. Six long months of what felt like torture. "It's like I'm stuck in hell." I reiterated, my voice weak from exhaustion. It had been about three months since I'd seen either of them. I couldn't get out of the house; it felt like something was forcing me back in every time I tried to leave. It was holding me hostage.

Kayla sighed when she looked at me for the first time in months. They showed up at my door and banged on it until I let them in. They had both come to confront me because I had basically been ignoring them. Everything inside me yelled at me to send them away; *they don't belong here; I don't need them.* But I knew better; I did need them. It was that thing telling me those things. When I opened the door and they saw me, all the anger on their faces drained, and they looked so concerned and scared for me. The last time they saw me, I looked a million times better. My hair was washed, I was a few pounds heavier, and I wasn't covered in bruises and scratches. "What the hell happened to you?" She looked ready to cry.

They dragged me out of the house, it hurt at first like someone was wringing their hands around my soul, but the further I got, the better I started to feel. I leaned into Brandon in the backseat, and I just started crying. It was the first time in months that I felt like myself. He just held me as we drove back to Kayla's place. She made me a cup of tea, and they sat me down and made me talk.

"You won't believe me," I whispered, hugging my knees to my chest and warming my hands on the cup. "It doesn't even seem real." But it was real, all of it.

"Lizzie, whatever happened, we need to know. If someone did this to you, we need to go to the police." She placed her hand on my knee as she tried to comfort me.

I shook my head. "You don't understand; it wasn't someone." I took a shaky breath. "It was something."

It sounded like a bomb had gone off. I jolted up in my bed and looked around the room, it was quiet, and the night was still. I guess I heard the sound in my dream and it scared me awake. I sighed and laid back down. Halfway back to sleep, I heard the next noise, one not easily written off: a scream from the floor below pulled me back out of sleep.

It didn't stop there; another scream and another, one on top of the next, moving downstairs. More screams and the sound of things being thrown and knocked down in the struggle. I could hear their shrieks moving down the hall. The glass from the photos cracked as they fell. I couldn't move; I could only sit there shaking as I heard those two girls get attacked in my house. A door banging against the wall made me jump out of my skin.

I could hear words now, "No, please, we'll be good, please!" Then a loud shriek as she was thrown down the basement stairs. The clambering of her body down on the concrete made me wince. The other girl wailed, and a man's voice rang through the house. He shouted in rage as the other girl was thrown down the stairs, and he slammed the basement door shut, making me flinch and a scared cry escaped my throat.

It was quiet then. I sat listening and shaking, trying to figure out what just happened. A pounding on my door made me scream again, then more and more—*bang, bang,*

*bang.* Someone was beating on my door, trying to get in. I could see the door shaking as someone's heavy fists tried to break it down. The man's voice from earlier started shouting again, "Let me in!" He yelled over and over. It went on forever; I couldn't move or breathe. I could only sit there and cry, holding myself and hoping it would all go away, go away, go away, "Go away!" I screamed at him.

Nothing. The banging stopped, and there was no more screaming—just the muted night. I couldn't sleep anymore. I just sat there and cried.

"When I went downstairs the next day, my photos were on the floor, my lamp was knocked off the table, and my bedroom door had marks on it." I took a long sip of my tea. "I couldn't figure out what the hell happened. I wasn't broken into; all the doors were still locked, and there weren't any poor girls in my basement." I sighed and looked down. "I had been having weird things happen for a couple of weeks at that point, but nothing so insane."

They were quiet for a moment; obviously, they didn't want to believe it. "Babe, what you're saying..." Branson started.

I scoffed, "I know it sounds crazy, but I have been living like this for months. And it just kept getting worse."

It's been almost three months since I've moved in. I've never been in so much constant pain. I've woken up with a new bruise or scratch for two weeks straight. Some weren't as nasty, just light bruises that hurt to the touch, but others looked like I got pelted with a bowling ball. The deep purple one on my hip hurt so bad I could barely walk around. I had to start working from home because of how bad it was getting; I could barely get out of bed some days.

The scratches were the same; some were light and grazed the skin, while others were deep. I'd wake up with blood running down my skin. It felt like I was being tortured each night. Around this time, I started to have the dreams, too. Well, night terrors would probably be a better description. These humanoid creatures were staring down at me, each taking their turn in torturing me. I couldn't scream or run away. I could only sit there as they took their time to cut me open.

Eventually, the dreams got worse. It was no longer just cutting me open; I could feel the things... violating me. Every night for weeks, I would be assaulted a hundred different ways in my nightmares, and I could still feel it when I woke up. I constantly had agonizing cramps, and I ended up with a UTI a week after the nightmares escalated.

I felt like my body was turning on me. I had no control over what was happening, and there wasn't anyone who could help; not like they would believe a ghost was attacking me. I couldn't get anything done outside the house because every time I stepped outside, I felt like every bruise and scratch was on fire. It was like someone put hooks into every infliction and used them to drag me back to the house. It made it difficult to go anywhere for too long.

Eventually, I didn't leave anymore. I was stuck in the house; I ordered all my groceries and anything else I needed. It wanted me to itself. Anytime I tried to contact my friends or Brandon, my phone or computer started going haywire and nothing would go through. I never received anything, and I couldn't send anything. I was completely isolated. It had me where it wanted me.

"That's why we haven't heard anything from you?" Brandon asked. I nodded, and he sighed. "I don't know... this all just sounds a little..."

"Crazy?" I suggested. I sniffed, not realizing I had started crying as I told them all this. "How do you think I've felt? I thought I was going insane, hearing things, seeing things, having insane nightmares. I thought I was going to die in that house. I know how crazy it sounds; I really do. But I don't have any other explanation."

We sat there silently for a moment as they took it all in. I finished my tea and set the cup on the table. "Why do you look so... gross?" Kayla asked. "Sorry, I couldn't think of another word."

I chuckled again. "No, I get it; I feel gross. I've been sick non-stop for the past couple of months, between the UTI and the horrible stomach pains. I've gotten some sort of flu-like thing, got stomach viruses, and thrown up more than I can eat. I've lost a crazy amount of weight because of it. Showering isn't fun." I hugged myself again. "I constantly felt like someone was watching me; I've felt hands on me. I've even seen someone in the bathroom. And it's every bathroom; I'm not safe in any of them. The last time I was able to take a shower, there was two weeks ago."

This was my least favorite part of the day. I hated trying to get a shower here; I hated the feeling of being watched, though I guess being watched is better than being touched. Sometimes it would be a graze on my leg or back; once, I felt someone touch my chest. I didn't use my main bathroom after that.

I turned on the water and waited until it was hot enough before quickly stripping down and getting in. The hot water burned the most recent cuts and felt slightly relieving on the bruises. I wanted to make this quick, not wanting to give the pervo ghost more than that. I could feel the stares as soon as I stripped down. *Just get through it, just get through it.*

I was washing my body when it happened. I felt a rush of wind behind me like someone opened a window. With the wind came the strong feeling that someone was there; goosebumps rose on my entire body, and my fight or flight told me to run as fast as possible. I froze, not wanting to turn around and see who was there. I continued washing my body and letting the water keep me warm, but the cold feeling was still behind me.

The feeling of a hand ran down my back. I gasped and froze in my spot again. The hand kept moving down my back, over my ass, and back up. A low grumbling sound rang close to my ear. My body ran cold, and I started shivering despite the heat of the water. It was like my nightmares: getting violated, and I couldn't do anything. I looked over slightly and saw something out of the corner of my eye through the clear shower curtain. I could see in the mirror someone behind me. It was a man; he looked older; his hair was grey, and his ash-like skin was wrinkling. He was still wearing clothes, and I could see his hand running over me.

It was too much. I screamed and swung my arms in his direction, trying to get him away. I pulled at the curtain and threw water around the room. I wanted him off; I couldn't stand him touching me anymore.

"When I looked over the documents, I saw that the man in the shower was Mr. Poole, the guy who ran the girl's home with his wife." I sniffed and wiped the tears from my eyes. "I couldn't shower again, not after that."

They were quiet. I wish I could make them believe, make them understand. "Lizzie, you're telling us you've been getting abused by a ghost," Kayla asked.

"Probably a couple. I think it was Mr. Poole, the original owner, and someone else, I don't know who, but I didn't recognize the face from the documents." I paused and watched their faces. "Look, I know this sounds crazy, but look at me; listen to me. Do I sound like I'm making this shit up? Do you really think I would lie about something like this?"

Brandon sighed. "No, it's insane, but you're not the type to freak out over nothing. I wish you would've come to us sooner, though."

"I wish I could've. The only reason I'm here is because you pulled me out of the house. I'm honestly surprised I'm not in pain right now. Maybe it's because you guys are with me, I don't know." I took a deep breath, the first freeing breath in months. "All I know is I'm not going back, at least not alone."

They looked at each other and then back at me. "You can move in with me. I don't know what you'll do with the house, though." Brandon offered, and I sighed with relief, knowing I didn't have to stay there anymore.

"I don't know, and I don't care. I can't stay there anymore." Brandon maneuvered us so he could hold me on his lap. "I can't go back there alone."

He kissed the top of my head. "Don't worry; you won't."

All my stuff was moved out of the house and into Brandon's within a week. I was never in the house alone; Brandon, Kayla, or my parents were always with me. I told my parents what had happened, and I could tell my dad had this "I told you so" look, but he didn't say any-thing.

I sat with Brandon on the couch after all the stuff was finally moved. It's only been a little over a week, and I felt so much better. No more bruises and scratches, no more horrible dreams, and I've been well enough to eat and start returning to a healthy weight. "Thank you," I said to him as we cuddled. "I think you saved my life."

He chuckled and kissed my head. "No need to thank me, baby." He was quiet for a second. "I think I saw some-thing while I was there." I looked up, surprised. "I wasn't sure what to think of it. It was that day I was there by myself. I was packing the stuff in your bedroom and heard something downstairs. I headed down to see if Kayla or your dad had come by, but there wasn't anyone there. I checked around, but I couldn't find anything. I was going to go back upstairs, but I saw a man standing at the top of the stairs. I blinked, and he was gone, but I could feel eyes on me the rest of the night. It was creepy as hell."

I chuckled. "Told you." It felt good that he saw something as well.

"Yeah, yeah. Let's get to bed." He pulled me from the couch, and we headed to our room. I still worry about having those night terrors, but since leaving that nightmare house, I've had nothing but sweet dreams.

# THE SHIVER

I don't understand why I'm shivering so much; the air conditioner is set to 68, and it's been a warm spring. Yet, I'm shivering as if I had walked into a freezer. Maybe I should go see a doctor; something must be wrong with my nerves. Even as I sit with a blanket around me on the couch, they won't stop.

They've been going for an hour, wracking through my body, and making me feel sore from the tension. As my husband came into the house, though, they had calmed down, and I was able to relax. It's like my body only found comfort from his presence. The idea made me sigh. We've been having trouble the last few months, constantly arguing over nothing. It's like almost every-thing we talk about turns into an argument. It scares me because I love my husband, I've loved him since we were in high school, and I don't want to lose him over silly things.

He had taken to working in the backyard to calm himself, it's become his happy place, and it makes me feel a little better knowing he has a healthy vise instead of drinking, or worse. When he walks in, his grey shirt is darkened with sweat, and his hair hangs in his face. He grabs a bottle of water from the fridge and downs it. When he sees me curled up with a blanket he gets a curious look on his face. "It's almost 80 degrees out, why are you in under a blanket?" He asks with a laugh. It makes me feel better, knowing our conversation isn't starting with an argument.

I shrug and push it down a bit now that the shivers have subsided. "I've been shivering like crazy the last few months. It'll last for hours sometimes and then go away for a while and return. I'm thinking about going to a doctor about it; something must be wrong."

He walks over and presses a warm hand to my forehead; it's such a comforting touch, I close my eyes and lean into it. "You don't feel sick; I'm sure it's nothing." He pulls his hand away and returns to the kitchen quicker than I could gather myself. He said it so carelessly. I remember he used to bend over backward if I so much as coughed.

"I just want to make sure, you know? Doesn't hurt to check." I stand and follow him to the kitchen. "I was thinking we should order out tonight. Chinese sound good?" I smile at my husband and lean across the island between us.

He huffs out a sigh, and I feel my heart sink. "Like we have the money to order out all the time." He bites back and takes another swig of water. "Just cook whatever we have."

I pull back and frown. "I mean, we haven't ordered out in a while, and I just got my raise, so we'll have more income." I walk around the island and wrap my arms around his waist, hoping the affection will keep him from starting an argument. "Just tonight?" I pout up at him, adding a playful edge to my voice.

But he rolls his eyes and pulls away from me, "Whatever, you can never just do as I ask, can you?" He scoffs and starts back out the back door.

"Can we please not argue anymore? Why do you keep getting upset with me?" I can't help the outburst. I've been dealing with this for months now, and I don't know how to make it better. "Do you not love me anymore?" It's a horrible thought, but what else could it be?

He groans and turns back to me, annoyance becoming a permanent fixture on his face. "Maybe if you were smart about things, and maybe if you weren't bothering me all the time, I wouldn't be mad at you." He sighs and shakes his head. "I work so hard around this house; all I ever hear you do is complain, whine, and push at my nerves. I ask you to do simple things, and suddenly it's a chore. Do something right for once, then maybe I won't get upset." His voice rose as he spoke. Each word cut deep into me. I notice he didn't answer my last question.

"I'm not trying to make everything an argument. Every time I ask you something or bring something up, it's like I offended you to your core. I can't even kiss you anymore without it seeming to piss you off." My eyes blur; I hate it when I cry in front of him. It's another reminder that he no longer cares. "If you don't want to be with me anymore, just say it. I'm tired of feeling like you don't care anymore."

He sighs again and rolls his eyes. "You always play such a victim; I'm not the bad guy here, Mary."

"Then answer me. Do you love me?" He stands there and glares at me. He still doesn't speak as he leaves out the back door and slams it shut. As he leaves, another wave of shivers runs through me. Though I feel this time, it may be caused by the painful sob that rips through me. I lost my husband, my high school sweetheart, and I don't know what I did or what to do.

At my mother's house a week later, I sit shivering, holding a cup of tea, and crying to my mom like a teen-ager. She's surprised to find out how much of a dick Henry has turned into. She had been so excited when we got married a year ago. She had been there with us as we cried over my infertility. "Do you think it's because I can't have kids? He only started acting like this shortly after finding out."

My mother scoffs over her cup, "If he is willing to throw away your entire relationship because of that by acting like an asshole, you deserve better." She shakes her head and reaches out to grab my hand. "If you don't think it's going to get any better, it's best just to leave and get it over with than to put yourself through that much pain." I sigh, upset that I can't help but agree. If he doesn't stop and continues to make me feel as bad as I do, I can't put up with it anymore.

I get home later in the night to find Henry sitting on the couch, drinking a beer. "Henry?" I ask softly, scared he'll get annoyed just by my presence. He hums in response and looks back at me. He doesn't look annoyed yet, but I know I was about to get those looks and probably worse. I take a deep, shaking breath. "I need to talk to you about something important, and I really don't want this to be an argument."

He raises his eyebrow at the statement but doesn't say anything. I walk around the couch to sit on the chair perpendicular to it. I don't say anything for a moment, trying to sort out my thoughts and gather my courage. "Well?" He asks, his tone gaining that edge.

I look at him in his eyes, "I don't know what happened to us. I don't know what has torn us apart. I mean, I guess it must be because I can't have kids because you've seemed to have hated me since we found out." At the mention of my infertility, he sucks in a breath but keeps quiet. "I love you so much, and I wish I could give you kids; I wish I could have them; I really do. I mean, there are other options, and I'd love to have a family with you; that's what I've always wanted." I pause, feeling the tears build up. I sniff but won't let them stop me. "But I have felt so unloved these last few months. I want so badly to work this out, and get past this, to go back to how things were. I wish you would kiss me good morning again and hold me when I cry like you always have. I wish I could figure out how to make you love me again. But if we can't fix this, then I think it would be best if I just left."

He doesn't speak; he sits there taking deep breaths like he's calming himself down. He seems to be thinking about what I said. I wait, praying he would realize how shitty he's been and turn things around. When he remained quiet for longer than expected, I took the silence as my answer. I nod, feeling my heart fall into my gut. I stand, ready to walk away and pack my things. Ready to leave a large portion of my life behind. Until he grabs my wrists, stopping me in my tracks. It isn't aggressive like I expected it to be, it's soft, and I feel his thumb rub against my skin.

When I look down at him, he has a face I haven't seen in a long time; he's hurt. He seems sad at my declaration, heartbroken almost, and for the first time in months, I feel hopeful that this would turn around. "I'm sorry, Mary." His voice is strained. "I don't know what happened; it was like one day I woke up, and everything angered me. I felt like everything in the world was against me, and I took all of it out on you. I think finding out about you made everything worse. It was like the world was giving me a big fuck you." He sighs and gently pulls me down to sit next to him. "I still feel angry, and I don't know what to do. But I don't want to lose you. I love you."

I sob, hearing those words for the first time in forever, and pull him into a tight hug. He returns it, and we hold each other tightly, afraid to ruin the moment. The relief washes over me like a tidal wave. "We can work it out; we can get help. I know you don't like the idea of therapy, but I think we both need it right now. I think it may help." He sighs in my ear, and I brace myself for an argument, but it never comes; instead, he agrees. I smile into his shoulder, ready to get this new step in our journey taken care of.

It's been two weeks since our conversation, and things have gotten so much better. He has returned to morning kisses and casual touches. He no longer starts fights; we even went out for date night. We started seeing a couple's therapist; he was a little apprehensive but eventually agreed. I feel so much peace.

I keep shivering, though, and they seem to be getting worse. I can barely stand with how hard they shake my body whenever I have a fit. The doctors can't seem to figure out what's causing it. All the tests they ran had come back normal, so they think it's all in my head. I could understand the shivers back when Henry and I were fighting, but now that we're getting better, I don't understand. I brought it up to our therapist during an independent session; she said it may be stress, and even though our relationship is working out again, the stress of working on the relationship is causing the shivers. I didn't really understand it.

It's Friday night, and a few coworkers and I decided to go out and have a few drinks. Henry texts me a few times to check in on me, but he hasn't gotten aggressive like he used to. He hated it when I would stay out late with my friends. Now he just texts me to stay safe, and that he was going to work on the little gazebo he's been building.

I wish I can enjoy dinner, but I can't stop shivering; my body shakes with the strength of an earthquake. The girls are concerned for me as I can barely hold a conversation. They ask what's wrong if I'm sick, and what's happening. I explain that I've been getting shivering episodes for months now. I'll get them for hours at a time then they'll be gone. It's been getting worse the last few days, but the doctors say I'm fine.

"Well, maybe someone's dancing on your future grave." One of the girls laughs while sipping her cocktail. I turn up an eyebrow at her. "Well, you know what they say, whenever you get a shiver, someone is walking on your future grave." She shrugs and giggles, the alcohol hitting her a bit.

I shake my head at her antics, an old superstition. "What's your husband up to?" One of the others asks.

Through the shivers, I answer, "He's working in the backyard. He's been doing that a lot the last couple of months; it's been kind of his coping mechanism." I take a sip from my drink, the tinge of alcohol burning ever so slightly. "We've been fighting a lot, but we've been getting better the last few weeks." I smile, thinking of how my husband has turned around.

Jillian giggles from the alcohol. "Yeah, maybe that's where the shivers come from, him working on the yard." She wiggles her fingers and makes a ghost-like sound. My eyes shoot open in shock; how drunk is she to think such an awful thing? My backyard as my grave? Ridiculous!

For some reason, though, I can't get my mind to turn away from it. I keep thinking back to all the episodes. They've always been during the weekend or in the afternoon after work, all the times Henry would be outside.

And when he would come inside, the shivering stopped. I scoff at myself. How ridiculous am I to think such an insane superstition is real? I force my mind off the subject and let myself return to the conversation. At around seven, the shivers stop, and I get a text from my husband that he's going to bed and to get home safely.

I get home at a quarter after eight. The house is quiet and dark. I sigh, feeling tired, but other things are pulling at my brain. For some reason, what Jillian had said stuck inside my head. Why would it be, though? It's not like the backyard could be my future grave; if that were the case, I would have been shivering since we moved in a year ago. It's ludicrous. Yet, I still find myself walking out the back door and looking over the yard.

Henry has done an amazing job. He had built a new deck, planted beautiful flowerbeds, and was starting work on a little gazebo. I'm excited to see how it turns out; I can picture sitting on a little porch swing reading a book as Henry grills on the deck. Maybe we can get a dog; it might help us get closer. He hasn't had a dog since we were 14, but he loves them. I'll ask him tomorrow to see how he feels about it.

I walk over to the area he had dug out for the gazebo. I don't get any shivers, only furthering the proof that what Jillian said was just a story. He had dug a deep hole, about seven feet wide and five feet deep. It's much deeper than I thought it needed to be, but Henry is the builder, so he knows best. The warm wind runs through the trees, yet somehow I still shiver as though it's cold. "Mary." I jump and turn to see Henry coming towards me. "What are you doing?" Why does he sound so accusatory?

I smile, but the shiver keeps up and worsens the closer he steps. "I was just checking out your work. I'm excited to see it finished." I keep my face smiling, but the coincidence of the shivering starting as soon as he came out is too unreal.

I watch him swallow, and his eyes dart to the hole he dug. "It's not safe out here; you should come inside." Why does he look so nervous? Maybe he just looks tired. I did have a couple of drinks, so I might just be confused. I nod and fall into step with him, and he pulls me back into the house, the shivers stopping as we walk in.

I had the weirdest dream. At least, I think it was a dream. I had tossed around in my bed, feeling Henry's side was empty. When I opened my eyes, I could make out a figure at the end of the bed; it was Henry. He was staring down at me; that old look of annoyance and hatred was back. His fists were balled up, and I noticed an object in one hand, but I couldn't make out what it was. "Henry?" I mumbled, still half-asleep, and sat up a bit.

In an instant, his expression changed back to the loving husband I knew, and his hands went behind his back. "Go back to sleep, baby." He whispered, and I was too tired to argue.

When I wake up again, Henry is in the kitchen making breakfast. I greet him as I join him, and he seems completely normal; he doesn't mention anything about last night, so it must have been a dream. We have no plans today, and Henry is taking a break from yard work to spend time with me. It's nice; we start a new show and catch up on all the things we may have missed during the time we were fighting. I bring up the idea of getting a dog eventually. He frowns at first, and I feel he is going to argue, but he takes a deep breath and smiles. "We can talk about it." I smile brightly, happy that we're getting back to normal. I don't even have an episode today.

After dinner, I feel lightheaded. It comes on suddenly, and I grab my head as it spins. "What's wrong?" Henry's concerned voice breaks through the spinning, and his warm arms hold me in place.

"I just feel really dizzy. Maybe I should go lie down." I feel like I'm mumbling, not able to really put any words together. He pulls me to my feet and helps me get up to bed. He's so sweet, helping me get comfortable and kissing my forehead before sleep takes over.

I wake up feeling nauseous; my head spins and throbs behind my eyes. I groan and turn over, expecting my soft pillow, but instead, I inhale rough dirt. I cough and finally open my eyes. It's dark; the only light I can see is the moon above me, encircled by the top of the hole I'm in. The ground is rough and warm from the earlier sun. I try to understand what's going on, where am I, and how did I get here? I try to move but find my body is wrapped tightly in course ropes that bind my arms to my side and my legs together. A whimper escapes me as fear takes over.

"Henry!" I call out for help; I need my husband; I need help! I continue to cry out as tears fall down my face. My body shakes as I try to catch my breath in the panic.

"I thought you would be asleep longer." A voice comes from above me, and I turn to it. "No, you had to wake up and make this harder." It's Henry, but his voice isn't his; it sounds like him, but it's cold and flat. "You never can do anything right, can you?"

I sob, "H-Henry, what are you doing? Let me out, please." I wiggle and try to break free but to no use. "This isn't funny; let me out."

He jumps down into the hole I'm stuck in and kneels by me, the smell of his sweat and cologne stinging my nose. "Why would I do that?"

I cry harder, the realization of what's happening hitting me harder than a train. He has been lying to me all along, he wasn't getting better, and we weren't work-ing things out. He tricked me into staying so he could kill me. "Henry, why? Why?" I cry, trying to see his face in the dark, hoping it's just an impersonator, not my husband.

He cocks his head, and I hear him sigh. "You don't deserve to live. You don't deserve to keep living a happy life. You're so worthless you can't even have my kids. I've put up with all your bullshit for years, and you can't even do that for me?" He scoffs. "Then to think you could just leave me. Just up and walk away because you were a little sad. Boo-hoo." He mocks me, and I can't stop sobbing. "Shut up." He growls.

I can't stop, though; he's been lying to me my whole life, fooling me into loving him. He's always been so kind and loving; where did this come from? "This isn't you, Henry; please, you wouldn't do this. Please let me go." I beg; his laugh above me shakes me to my core.

"You have no idea who I am." It's the last thing he says before hopping out of the hole. I cry out, screaming for help, trying to get the attention of the neighbors. My whole life blurs in front of my eyes, breaking me into pieces, realizing it was all a lie. "Goodbye, Mary." His voice hits my ears before the shovel does, and the world goes dark.

# RED EYES

Ever since I was little, I've been afraid of the dark. The claustrophobia of not knowing what's right in front of me sends panic throughout my veins. I despise the idea of being unable to see, of being surrounded by who knows what and not even knowing. There's too much at risk when left in a room with no light. The one I think of is explicitly from my worst nightmares, a creature so horrendous that I still fear it even after twenty years. Whenever I get trapped in a black room, I'm afraid I'll see those red eyes again.

I was too young to remember most of the details of my daily life. I remember having fun at school and enjoying all the holidays when I got to dress up or receive presents. I remember the very first house I ever lived in. My sister and I started our lives in this house, the home that began my family. To the rest of the world, it was a cute rancher with a wrap-around porch, and a large backyard, a perfect family home. I remember the tall tree that hung over the front lawn and gave us plenty of leaves in the fall to play with. I can still picture the dark brick and shingles that made up the exterior.

The inside was comfortable and homey. It was long, with our playroom and the office in the front, leading to the living room, and through a doorway was our quant kitchen. A short hallway to the left of the living room led to my parent's room on one end and a room I shared with my sister on the other. On the back end of the kitchen was a door that led down into the basement.

The basement was the worst part of the house. It was a long basement with a concrete floor and three or four hanging lightbulbs. The laundry room was just off to the right, a few feet from the stairs. Only a few windows at the top of the walls let in a little bit of light during the day. It would be pitch black at night until you walked a few feet from the stairs to turn on the first hanging bulb. To the unknown eye, it was an average unfinished base-ment. It held all our unused items, storage, and old things that were handed down to us.

It was a weird room, even to a five-year-old. I always hated going down there, even during the day. There was a smell that always made me want to gag; I could never figure out what it was. I thought it was rotten eggs or a dead skunk, but nothing could ever come close to describing it. I had to hold my breath most of the time to keep myself from throwing up. I seemed to be the only one who could smell it. I asked my mom multiple times if she could smell it, too, but her answer was always no.

While the smell was bad and the dark made it ominous and unwelcoming, they were not the strangest things about the basement. What looked like a bedroom was set up on the back end of the room, shadowed from any daylight as there weren't any windows there. It was something out of a Victorian bedroom; an old wire frame bed with old dusty covers, a bedside table complete with a lamp that didn't work, and a dresser to the right stacked with old boxes and filled with things I can't remember. A wardrobe sat in the corner; I don't know what was in it - if there was anything at all. I never dared to open it, afraid to see what may have been inside. My parents said they were old pieces of furniture from my mom's childhood. I don't believe I ever got a straight answer on why we kept it if it was just going to sit and collect dust. I guess it was for the sentimental value. Either way, looking at it made my skin crawl.

My parents never really listened to or believed me when I told them what was down there. It wasn't just the storage, the old Christmas décor, and the random bedroom set-up. There was something dark down there that scared the shit out of me. It haunted my dreams and terrorized me while I was awake. For a while, I was only safe during the day, it didn't seem to like daylight, but I guess most demons don't. That's what I figured out it was, now that I'm old enough to understand.

I still see its face when my nightmares turn dark. Its image has been permanently engraved into my mind, assaulting me when I have a moment of peace and reminding me that it's still there. It had black and red skin, but it didn't look like skin; it was like rocks and rubble packed together to make a body. Veins of red break through the rocky black surface, almost volcanic. It had thick arms with hands that had long sharp claws.

They extended longer than usual fingers, sharpened to a point like a needle. Its face, God, that face. That skull-like face. Where its lips should've been were just large fangs leading to a hollow mouth. It had no nose, just two gaps in its face. Its eyes were large and solid red with no pupils or whites, just red, burning into me for the rest of my existence. Its chin came to a narrow point, and the top of its head looked like a thorn bush made of rock. Horns tangled among themselves with sharp ends pointing in every direction. I would constantly draw it and show my parents, but they just thought I had a wild imagination.

Every time I went into that basement, I saw it. Even during the day, when I thought it was safe, I could still see those eyes staring down at me. It hid in the back of the basement, where the wardrobe stood. It was like it took claim of the bedroom space. I would go down to grab something, like my snow sled or summer clothes, and I could smell it, see it, and hear that awful growl from the back of the room. That deep rumble resonated in my chest and vibrated my brain until I felt like bugs were crawling underneath my skin. My head throbbed every time I set foot on that concrete floor. I didn't know what it had against me. I thought it was because I was the only one who could see it; maybe it didn't like that. I know now it had wanted me – my young, innocent soul; it let me see it so it could feed on my fear. Why else would everyone in my family be safe from the rancid smell, the terror, all of it?

I thought I may have been crazy; no one believed me, and my parents thought I was imagining things. They didn't understand how real everything was, how I felt like my life was in mortal danger daily. I would tell them about the nightmares and the red eyes, but they would pat my head and laugh about my inventiveness. They constantly praised me for being an excellent storyteller. I wish they had listened to me then.

One warm night, my mom asked me to grab the laundry from the basement. I didn't want to, though; I told her I hated the basement; it was too dark and scary. But she was busy and needed my help; she needed me to be a brave girl. "It's just dark for a second," she told me, "turn on the light, and it'll be okay. The scary things can't get you; they aren't there." I argued and whined; I didn't want to go down there. She had enough and said I would be in trouble if I didn't. I didn't want to be in trouble, so I had to go.

I took a deep breath and opened the door. The air was warm, but a shiver ran over me as I descended the concrete stairway. The concrete felt like ice on my bare feet. I relied on the light from the kitchen to see my way down into the darkness, but it soon became too far, and my eyes were left to try to adjust to the blackness that surrounded me. There was something different when I went down that time. The sinking feeling in my chest halted my movement before I reached the last step. The air was thick, and my stomach heaved from the rancid smell that engulfed me. I couldn't see it, but the growling was closer, louder than it usually was. Where it normally came from the far end, it now echoed a few feet before me. My heart was pounding in my tiny chest as I looked around, trying to see the source and gauge how close it was. *Do I have time to run to the light? Should I turn back? I'll get in trouble if I turn back.* All of these thoughts ran through my mind as fear quaked through me.

I tried to get to the light; I ran forward to where I knew it was, but I didn't make it. I felt something hot on my face, much hotter than the late spring night. The rotten smell scorched my lungs, causing me to fall back. I hit the ground hard, but my fear urged me up and forced me to run back to the stairs as quickly as possible. I didn't want to see what the thing had planned for me. It had never gotten that close before, to where I could feel its breath on my face. I was so glad it was dark then because I couldn't see its face up close.

I ran up towards the dim light at the top of the stairs, reaching towards my salvation, but it was yanked away from me as I was pulled by my ankle back down the stairs. I cried out in fear and pain as I tripped forward and grappled at the stairs before my face fell into them. I pulled my leg from whatever had grabbed it and ran back up the stairs, crying. My mom met me at the top, wondering what happened and why I was crying. She asked me if I had tripped or hit something. She wouldn't believe me if I told her; she never did. I just sat there crying hysterically on her shoulder as she held me in the kitchen. I couldn't explain it to her or my dad; they would say I was imagining it, like always. Though, I couldn't imagine the bright red scratches across my ankle. Three thick, painful welts marked my tiny ankle and stung with every step I took. I couldn't imagine that, and I know Mom couldn't, either, even if she didn't want to believe the reason behind them.

Since that day, I refused to go into the basement. Anytime my parents asked me to get something I declined and stood my ground, no matter how much trouble I got into. After a while, they stopped asking; they understood that there was something I was terrified of. They didn't fully comprehend why, but I didn't have to go down there again. I felt happy for a while; I didn't have to go into the beast's lair like bait. But I still couldn't get away from it.

Since I wasn't going down to it, it seemed to take its time coming to me. First, it attacked my dreams; I had nightmares all the time. It was always there chasing me, hurting me. Things a five-year-old couldn't possibly imagine warped into my mind and terrorized me repeatedly. I could feel the searing pain from my dreams even when I woke up: the stabbing of its clawed fingers into my chest, trying to dig out my heart, the burn of fire licking against my skin and melting my flesh, my eyes and tongue being ripped from my face. I would wake up screaming and crying every night for months. My parents were worried, I knew they were, but they didn't know how to take care of it. They didn't know who to contact; the psychiatrist said it was just regular night terrors. There isn't much to be done about night terrors. When I told him about the demon in the basement, he told me that my imagination was quite adventurous.

It only left me alone when my parents let me sleep with them, but that wasn't as often as I would've liked.

After a few months, I stopped sleeping. I couldn't close my eyes without seeing that face and those blood-red eyes. I became an insomniac at six years old because of that monster. My doctor didn't understand it; my parents were stressed over my health. I became a shell of who I used to be. The only time I could get any sleep was nap time at school or when I stayed with my grandparents. It didn't take long for it to up its game again. It couldn't get me in the basement or my dreams, so it had to come up to me itself.

It was the middle of the night; I was watching something on the old box TV in my room. My sister was fast asleep; it was a rule that I had to keep the TV low so I wouldn't wake her if I couldn't sleep. I can still remember the room clearly. Our bunk beds sat on the wall with the door, our dressers and toys opposite the beds, and the little TV next to the large closet with sliding mirror doors. I hated those mirror doors; they squeaked too much when I opened them and hurt my ears.

It was a calm night; I was relaxing, and I felt it would be peaceful. My heart nearly stopped when I heard the nauseating squeak of the mirror door. I looked from the TV to the closet, and sure enough, the left side door was inching open. I moved under the covers, where I could be safe. My breath was shallow as my heart pounded in my chest. The soft sound of the TV still played but was overshadowed by the squeaking of the door. I started to smell it then, that rotting smell it gives off. I wanted to cry out but didn't want it to hear me; I was under the covers and safe. That's what 6-year-old me thought, as most young children do. I could hear my young sister still sleeping soundly above me, the noises having no effect on her.

I felt the heat before I heard anything else, like that day in the basement. It seeped through the blankets above my face and made me gag. A guttural growl accompanied the hot breath. The sound was inches from my face, causing my whole body to shake and small whimpers to escape, no matter how hard I tried to be quiet. I felt at that moment that I was going to die. I felt like it would fulfill everything it put in my dreams: tear me apart and eat me shred by shred. The moment I felt the pressure, the heaviness bearing down on my chest like he was ready to crush me under his hand, I couldn't hold in the screams anymore. They were blood-curtailing, fueled by the fear of being murdered and my soul being dragged to hell. I screamed and thrashed, trying to get it off me for what felt like forever. My limbs hit things, but I couldn't tell if they were the bed or its body. I felt his hold on me tighten, constricting my lungs, before disappearing completely when my mom ran into the room.

There wasn't any amount of comfort that could console me that night. I clung to her all night crying and shaking. My dad looked around the room like he would find a living man, but there was no evidence of an invader. Only a smear on the mirror, too high for my sister or me to reach. I couldn't go back to sleep, not that night or the night after. I refused to sleep in my room again. I had a permanent place in my parents' bed; even then, I couldn't sleep. I couldn't do anything without fear of that thing being there to kill me. I didn't want to go back to the house anymore. I was starting to feel like a prisoner in my own home. School and my grandparents' house were like safe havens. I started sleeping over at their house more and more to feel safe.

It was a relief when my parents told me we were moving when I was in the middle of second grade. I finally felt like I was getting out of this pit of despair. I was packing everything before anyone else; my toys and clothes were all in boxes before my parents even thought about booking a moving van. I was ready to get out of that house and escape that thing. I was excited to finally be safe. After so many years, I was finally able to get away. It was exhilarating; the fear of the night didn't bother me anymore as I looked toward the light of a new beginning.

The new house was great; it was quiet and felt like a breath of fresh air. No rotting smell or growling kept me up, and the nightmares finally ended. I was able to sleep in my own room for the first time in months; I wasn't worried about something grabbing me, and I slept peacefully. I started feeling more myself again now that I was well-rested and didn't have to look over my shoulder every night. I was still afraid of the dark; to this day, I still need a light on when I'm sleeping. There will always be that fear that, maybe, it decided to follow me.

It took some time before I could really talk to my parents about everything that happened. I was in my teens when we finally sat and talked. I explained everything I had gone through and told them I wasn't imagining it and feared for my life. During our talk, I discovered that my dad had some experiences in that house. He said nothing happened until I was born. After that, there were moments when he would hear things or find things around the house astray like a picture moved or a door opened. We used to have this big St. Bernard dog, a giant teddy bear, but he was our protector. My dad told me he was always scared to go into the kitchen; we had to feed him in the living room. He told me that one night after everyone had gone to bed, he was lying on the couch watching TV with the dog. Suddenly, he got up and started growling at the doorway.

My dad tried to get him to calm down, but he kept growling, the fur on his back raised, and his teeth bared at the empty doorway. He was about to get up and see what he was growling at when he yelped and ran back to my dad. He was no longer the protector of the house; he was crying and shaking as he barreled over my dad. As my dad tried to comfort him, he noticed a long bleeding cut on his face. *How the hell did that get there?* Was all he could ask. It freaked him out because it reminded him of when I got hurt in the basement. I think this was when he started making the connection and realized something terrible was there.

I was a little angry then because he had never believed me, even though he was also experiencing things. He told me it wasn't that he didn't believe me, but he didn't want to scare me more. But now that I know, even though I was angry, I felt better; I felt like I wasn't crazy. Knowing it was real and that I wasn't the only one who had to deal with it made me feel so much better. I felt free.

# THE DELIVERY



I never thought I would be on the cover of every newspaper. If I somehow did end up there, I would have hoped it would've been for something randomly heroic, you know, like saving a family from a fire or talking someone off the ledge. Maybe I would one day even win the lottery, and that's how I ended up in the papers with my face plastered all over the news. Never in a million years would I have thought it would revolve around something so horrifying.

It was a great day; it was one of those summer days that wasn't so hot it was unbearable, and the breeze kept everyone cool. The arts festival was going on its third and last day. I was hired to be the festival's photographer. I went around to the different booths and displays, taking pictures to put up on the festival's website. I also took the time to help the vendors and staff; I would take lunch orders or help with trash and make deliveries across the festival grounds. I like helping people, and it never took away from my photography gig.

The festival was slower on the last day, most people came on Saturday, but this day was the second busiest.

There were a lot of familiar faces, many of whom had been a part of the festival for years. It was a little weird that a couple of vendors weren't here today. It was a rule that you had to be here all three days, or you wouldn't be invited back. I've counted probably five or six vendors that were here yesterday but not today. They had some good products, too, so it's a shame they didn't stay.

There was something different about today; I couldn't really place my finger on it, though. Maybe it was the missing vendors or something. I ignored the feeling, though; I wasn't going to let anything ruin the last day of the festival. I took pictures of the award cere-monies and the kids enjoying their crafting activities. During my downtime, a few people asked me for some assistance, such as delivering products or ordering their lunch. I was excited to get some business requests from some vendors, either asking for photoshoots or editing work. That's one of the reasons I do the festival photog-raphy, everyone got to see my work in action, and I got a lot of business from it.

It was getting close to the end of the day; I was get-ting ready to start packing up when I felt a tap on my shoulder. I turned around and was faced with a man. He had salt-and-pepper hair and thin glasses; he was on the shorter end, probably about 5'8; he looked like a profes-sor, but he didn't work at the college, not that I know of. I've seen him around the festival a few times all week-end. I think he was a buyer, or maybe he worked with one of the vendors. There was something about him, though, that gave me a weird vibe.

He smiled as he greeted me. "Hello, my name is Austin; I'm a friend of one of the vendors here. He told me that you have been really helpful in doing deliveries around the festival. I was wondering if you wouldn't mind delivering this letter for him?" He produced a small white envelope from his back pocket and held it out. "I would do it myself, but he asked me to help him break down his booth." He shrugged with a chuckle.

I didn't know why, but something in the back of my mind said not to, but that's just silly; there was no reason to feel weird right now. I smiled and nodded. "Sure, where am I taking it?" I grabbed the envelope and looked at it. There was an address on the front.

"The address written there, it's a client of his. It's maybe two miles down the road if you still don't mind." He pulled out some cash from his pocket. "I know it's off festival grounds, so we'd happily pay you to take it." His smile reminded me of the Cheshire cat, wide and eerie. It stretched too far on his face, and rather than his eyes squinting with the movement, they remained wide open.

I kept my smile, though it felt a bit forced, "It's no problem. I was leaving for the day anyway, so I can head there on my way home." He pushed the money into my hand and thanked me for the help before walking away. I studied the address written on the envelope. Wilker's Road was one of those back roads with almost no one living on it; what kind of client lived out there? There are a lot of ghost stories around that road. Some say that if you go down the road at night by yourself, you'll never return. There have been some missing person reports around the area, but no bodies were ever found, so nobody investigated it much more than that.

Something felt a bit wrong, though. The letter felt odd in my hands, but I couldn't figure out why. I just shook my head; I was being ridiculous. *There's no need to feel weird; it's just a normal delivery. The guy was even nice enough to pay me for it.* I stuck the letter and the cash in my bag and went to my car. I put the address in my GPS and followed the directions. I usually didn't drive down Wilker's Road; it's never been on any of my routes. The two-way road was surrounded by thick trees that formed a canopy overhead. I checked the GPS to make sure I was going the right way. It said I had another two miles down this road, and the house would be on the right.

On the right side of the road, the trees disappeared and opened to a golden wheat field. I could just make out the green of the tree tops a few acres behind the tall crops. A few hundred feet down the road sat a dark barn house and a metal shed just to the right of it. It was a small house; most would likely glance over it as they drove by because it hid so well between the wheat fields on either side. There was a brown pickup truck that had to be a few decades old sitting in front of it, but there wasn't any other sign of life.

I pulled into the gravel driveway and stopped a few feet from the front door. When I got out, I could only hear the wind passing through the wheat. An uneasy feeling washed over me; I did not want to be here longer than I had to. I quickly went to the door and went to shove the letter into the mail slot when I heard some-thing other than the wind.

From the metal shed came the sound of a saw. I wouldn't have thought much of it had it not been for the scream that followed, then the nauseating sound of the saw cutting through something soft and fleshy. While I've never heard it in person, I've heard a similar sound in horror movies. There wasn't any more screaming as the saw continued. It wasn't safe here; I had to get out. I ran back to the car, thankful I kept it running, and sped back to the festival. My heart pounded in my chest as the sounds replayed in my head again and again. I couldn't help but picture what might have been on the other side of those metal walls.

Once I was safe back at the festival, I ran to the security tent where a few police officers sat. When I got there, I couldn't speak. I couldn't breathe; panic and fear took over every inch of my body. I shook and hyper-ventilated as they tried to calm me down enough to figure out what was wrong. At that moment, I realized the envelope was still clutched in my hand. I said noth-ing, just thrust the envelope into the closest officer's chest. He grabbed it, and I heard him open it.

"Maya? Hey, what's wrong? Are you okay?" A familiar voice breached through the buzzing of my panicked brain. I looked up to see my friend Zackary making his way towards me. "Breathe, breathe, Maya." He instructed and helped me calm down. It took a minute, but I could finally breathe and speak again.

"Ma'am, where did you get this? Who gave it to you?" The officer with the letter asked urgently.

"There was a man; he looked like a professor or something. He said he was friends with a vendor. He asked if I could deliver the letter to the address, and he said they were clients of his friend. I got there, oh god." The whining of the chainsaw rang through my skull. "I heard someone screaming, and there was a chainsaw." A sob worked its way out of my chest; I hadn't realized I was crying.

"Can you describe this man?" He pressed, holding my shoulder in what I guess was supposed to be a comforting gesture.

I nodded. "I have pictures of him from this weekend." The cop asked me to show him, and we spent the next few moments going through my camera and finding the ones with the best view of his face. "This is him." I pointed him out when he popped up. He was talking to one of the vendors that didn't show up today.

There was some static over one of the officer's walkie. "Chase to Donnelly, we've arrived at the residents in question. It's a nightmare here." I listened to them speak over the walkie. "Two suspects were found in the shed dismembering a human body. Upon further investigation, we found a meat freezer with at least a dozen bodies, some already dismembered, some intact. One suspect attacked the officers upon arrival and was shot dead. The other suspect has been arrested. We're bringing in backup to check out the rest of the property. Who knows how many more bodies there are?"

*Holy shit! I could've been hacked to bits; I could've died! That guy tried to send me to my death, and I went willingly. I knew something felt wrong, but did I listen to my instincts? No, I went to the murder house and almost got killed!* "Ma'am," the officer's voice brought me out of my spiraling. "We're going to need all the pictures from this weekend. We have reports that some of the guests and vendors this weekend had gone missing. It will be very helpful if we can try to match their pictures to the bodies." He spoke slowly and gently, trying not to scare me more than I already was. I nodded and handed him my camera bag with all my equipment and memory cards. "Thank you, you'll get this all back once we've gotten everything we need."

I nodded again and took a deep, shaking breath. "What did the letter say? Did it even say anything?" I couldn't help but wonder.

He drew his lips into a thin line. "I'm not sure it would be a good idea-"

"Please," I interrupted him. "I'd like to know."

He sighed. "It said, 'This is the last one I'm sending you today; pack her up for me.'" Hearing the message made me go numb for a moment; then, I was filled with so many questions. Who were these guys? Why were they doing this? Why me? I couldn't stop thinking about it all.

The man who gave me the letter was found and arrested a few days later. From what I could tell, they refused to answer any questions. They wouldn't tell the cops how many people they'd killed, but the police reported that a total of 37 different victims were kept in the meat locker. They're looking into all of the missing persons from the last couple of decades, just in case. But looking at the news and seeing my face with the headline "Local Artist Exposes Human Butchers" and giving so many families closure, and saving so many more lives, makes the answers all pointless in the end.

# THE SNOWMAN

It was a long winter and a frigid one. There were three massive blizzards and some flurries in between. It kept the ground covered all season. You get used to all the snow living so far north, you can't go a year without seeing it. My kids loved playing in the snow; they would have snowball fights and make snow angels and snowmen. One year they made a whole snow family, dog included, it was adorable, and they used some old food dye to make faces. It didn't feel much different this year.

It was a few days after the third blizzard when the news of little Jerrett came out. His poor family, I can't imagine how they felt. I read the news article and held my babies all night crying. Jerrett was friends with Tony, my oldest, they played mini league together the last two summers and were in the same classes. Lillian, my girl, always wanted to join in but she's six and they're eight, so it wasn't cool to be hanging out with a little girl; kids, you know?

After I heard the news, I went over to the Luxley's house and brought them some food; I know it wasn't much, but when you're looking for your son, you don't worry about food. I sat with them, and we had coffee and ate the lasagna I made. They told me Jerrett had gone out in the snow and never came back. He wanted to play and was actually headed over to my house to get Tony. I wasn't home at the time – Lillian was sick, so I took her to the doctor – but my husband was home with him. All I know was that he never made it to my house, neither my husband nor my son saw him that day. From what Jenny told me, Jerrett was wearing his bright red snowsuit, he shouldn't have been hard to miss in the white sea between our houses.

We were looking all over for him, and the added layers of snow weren't helping. We couldn't look too far into the woods, and there weren't any leads as to where he would've gone. The family couldn't think of anyone who may have taken him. Everyone in town was friends, we've barely had any crime and I couldn't think of anyone who would hurt a little kid. We didn't even have any sex offenders within a 5-mile radius, we had absolutely nothing to go on. It was heartbreaking, having to wait out the news of whether he was found or not.

Weeks went by, and still nothing. The local officers seemed like they wanted to give up on the investigation, which I get from their perspective, there were no leads, and we couldn't go searching too much into the woods due to the dangerous conditions. But as a mother, I couldn't believe them; I couldn't fathom how they would give up on a child. Everyone in town was outraged when they said they were going to stop investigating.

It had been about two months later when the snow

started to melt. We were all finally going to get answers; we could look around and get to the places we couldn't before. I was keeping the Luxley's company during all of this. I wanted to make sure they knew they had someone who was there for them, someone they could rely on. My husband took over caring for the kids. They were kept inside for the most part; we didn't want them going missing, too. When they were out, my husband was always with them. He was even helping them build the snowmen out back, ensuring they stayed in place and didn't melt away too much; the kids would've been upset, he would say.

That's how I usually found my husband when I came home; he was packing snow into the snowmen in the yard; there were three or four at a time. He was so good at keeping the little snow family together. It made me grateful to have my family, and then it made me feel guilty for being glad.

We had a weirdly hot day almost three months after the last big blizzard; it was warm enough that the grass was starting to peak out. It was time for the search party to look in the woods. It was the first thing everyone in town did. They all got together with their dogs and went out to look in the woods. My husband went with them, Jenny came over, and we all sat together. I had made some cookies, something calming to help with the anxiety. She had lost her baby three months ago, and I didn't know what else to do to comfort her, you know? All I kept thinking was that they would probably find his poor little body frozen somewhere; maybe he got lost following an animal and froze to death. I didn't want to think that, but those thoughts kept intruding.

At around three, I heard Lillian scream. Jenny and I rushed outside to see what was wrong, and she and Tony were standing with the snowmen in the backyard. They had been playing around and knocking them down to get a few snowballs out of them. The one in the middle, the largest, its head was knocked off, and something red was poking out of the top. I called the kids and told them to go inside.

I didn't want to think about it; I wanted to believe it was more food dye, but I knew we didn't have any more. I took a shaking breath, braved it, and knocked the snow away. I didn't know what to think then; I didn't have any thoughts in my head, really. How can you think when there's a dead kid hidden in a snowman in your yard?

I don't remember much of what happened after that. I know Jenny came running out, and there was more screaming. I think it was from her, and maybe there were some screams from me as well. Some time passed, I think, perhaps it was an hour, or no, it may have been a few minutes, and the police were there, too, and the ambulance as well. I know someone was talking to me, but I couldn't hear very well; I know I was holding someone, it may have been Jenny, and I think my kids, too. I'm sorry; like I said, everything became very fuzzy for a while.

I don't know how I never knew the poor boy was in my yard. I never could've thought something like this would've happened, not to us. I couldn't even comprehend that... that, I can't even think of it. I could never imagine that he could've done something like that. I mean, he never came home after the search party, and looking back, he spent way too much time working on those snowmen. He was hiding him; all this time and I never knew.

You said the boy was beaten, but that doesn't make sense; my husband has never laid a hand on anyone; he's never even raised his voice. He couldn't have beaten little Jerrett, not so bad that the poor thing would've died. My husband is a good man, a good father. I know how it all looks, he hid the boy, he ran, but I can't believe he killed him. This is too much.

End of Transcript, Statement of Miranda Trent, wife of Dylan Trent: Prime suspect of Jerrett Luxley's sexual assault and murder.

# THE DOLL

"I can't believe you actually took one of those creepy dolls." Sydney laughed at Ethan as he played with the tiny rag doll. It was an old flat doll with yellow yarn hair and an embroidered smile. Its little pink dress was old and tattered. It was probably cute to a normal person, but I thought it was just downright creepy.

"Ethan, why the hell would you take that thing? I don't want it in our house. I'm also pretty sure that's stealing." I scolded my idiot boyfriend. We were sitting in a booth at a local restaurant; it was busy, so we had to keep our voices down, meaning I couldn't properly yell at him for his idiocy.

"Come on, babe, it's cute." He held it up by its little hands and made it dance in the air. A shiver passed through my spine, seeing its creepy little eyes looking at me. "Besides, there are so many of those damn dolls there, they aren't going to notice if one is gone, right?" He sat the gross little thing next to him.

We had just come from a haunted tour of an old orphanage. It was built in the 1800s and ran for over a century. I had a lot of fun there. I love learning about specific pieces of history, and I love haunted history; I find it remarkably interesting. I had wanted to see the orphanage for a while. We live near a tourist town known for all its haunted histories, so there's a lot to explore. The orphanage was always booked, though, because it's one of the most haunted places in town.

It was intense walking around there. It was a five-floor building with a plethora of rooms for the children; there were bedrooms and classrooms, and there were quarantine rooms for the sick kids. There was so much to explore and learn that I wanted to stay there for as long as I could. I know, I'm the weird one who wants to stay in creepy places.

Though there was one room in the house I hated: the "doll room," which was a memorial for all the kids who lived there. There were so many dolls: porcelain dolls, stuffed animals, sock monkeys, and rag dolls like the one Ethan stole. I love creepy things, but I draw the line at dolls. However, seeing the hundreds of toys and thinking of all those kids was a little sad. Not all of them died, but there were many sicknesses during that time, and there were also a few wars that the town got caught in. The tour guide said more than half of the dolls represented a deceased child.

Another interesting thing to learn was how horrible the last caregiver was. Ms. Maisie Kelter was the caregiver for five years before she ended up getting the orphanage shut down. One of the last places on the tour was the basement, and I started crying while looking around. There were still chains and ropes hanging from the walls and ceilings. There were dark stains which I could only conclude were blood by the stories the guide told.

"Ms. Kelter, according to authorities at the time, was considered to be the actual devil. Many of the children who were in the orphanage ended up dying before they could get adopted. She starved them to the point that they would eat the rats running around. She would punish the children for so much as sneezing by bringing them down here and leaving them for days at a time; there were many times she would come down and find the child dead. She would then bury them in the grave-yard behind the building.

"Authorities were notified that something was going on because the graveyard groundskeeper found her burying three children. The authorities came in, looked around the building, and immediately sentenced her to hang. They saw all the abused kids, dead and alive, as well as the basement, and they got a hold of all the records she kept. It turned out that in the time she was the care-giver, over a hundred children had died and were buried in the cemetery."

It was rough listening to the story; some people in the world are so messed up. But learning the true history of the house was incredibly enlightening. After the tour, our little group of Ethan, Sydney, Victor, and I went to a restaurant we liked. This was where Ethan let us know he had stolen one of the dolls. "You know that probably belonged to a dead kid; you're really so immature that you stole a dead kid's doll?" I really could not believe he would do something like this.

"Oh, come on, Willow, it's not that big of a deal. It's a little souvenir; besides, it's not like the kid is using it anymore." He took a bite of his food and shrugged.

"It is a big deal, Dingus, you should never mess with things like that; did you want a ghost to follow us home? And you know how much I hate dolls." I crossed my arms and stared him down, not hungry anymore, even though the food in front of me smelled delicious.

"Will, you don't need to be so uptight about it; it's just a doll," Sydney said around her fries. Victor stays silent through this whole thing, just eating his food. He doesn't really like these haunted trips, but he comes with us because of Sydney.

"You don't have to have it in your house! Just because you don't believe ghosts are real doesn't mean they aren't, and you think bringing a dead kids doll from a haunted orphanage with a ghastly history into my house is okay?" They were really pissing me off, even if it wasn't about the haunted aspect; stealing a doll like that is so wrong.

"Will, chill, if it really upsets you, I'll take it back tomorrow." He shrugged again. I could hear the eye roll in his voice even if he didn't do it.

"Good." I finally took an angry bite of my food. I wish he could return it tonight, but they were already closed. I was not happy about having that thing in our house for the night.

I was still angry when we got home. Ethan would not

stop playing with the old doll and teasing me with it. Sydney and Victor went back to their house, and now I was stuck having to deal with this, not that my friends were any help. "Seriously, I don't get why you're so mad." Ethan threw the doll on the couch and followed me into the kitchen so I could grab some water.

"Because, Ethan, not only did you do something illegal, but you decided that the so-called 'humor' behind stealing the doll was more important than my comfort. You know I hate dolls, and you know how much I believe in that kind of stuff. I just wish you would have been more considerate." I crossed my arms and stared back at him.

He sighed and shoved his hands in his pockets; he at least had the decency to look somewhat sorry. "You're right. I'm sorry; I should have thought about what I was doing."

I nodded and walked past him. "You can think about what you did while you sleep down here with that thing." He started whining, but I shot him one of my famous death stares, and he conceded to my demands. "Good night, and I want that thing gone first thing in the morning," I stated and headed upstairs, ending the conversation.

Getting to bed was hard. I don't know why, but I couldn't sleep. Maybe it was because I knew there was a creepy ass doll in my house, or perhaps I just wasn't used to sleeping alone. I could deal with the latter; I hated this sickly feeling running through me. Ever since we got home, I'd just been annoyingly nauseous, not so much that I needed to get sick, but the feeling was enough to bother me. I rolled around, trying to get the feeling to go away, but it never did. I tried to drink the water I brought up, but it didn't help. *I can't be hungry, right? I had a large dinner, so I definitely shouldn't be hungry.*

It was about one in the morning at this point, I still couldn't fall asleep, and the nausea was getting worse. *Maybe a snack will help*, I concluded. I sighed and wrapped my long robe around me. I opened the bedroom door, and suddenly it felt ten degrees colder. *Did Ethan turn down the heat or something?* I wrapped the robe tighter and tiptoed down the stairs; I could hear Ethan's snores as I headed down. Once I got to the bottom of the stairs, I was freezing. I was shivering as I walked over to the thermostat. It read 52 degrees, but the temperature was set to 68. Why was it so cold? It was working fine earlier. I sighed and started walking to the kitchen.

I stopped and checked on Ethan, he was passed out on the couch, cocooned in blankets, but he seemed okay. I felt a little bad about making him sleep on the couch, but he seriously upset me this time. He knows better, and he usually wasn't like this; I don't know what had made him want to steal that doll. Speaking of, the creepy little thing was in the other chair. Ethan has such a weird sense of humor; he had set the thing up to look like it was sitting there. Its sewn eyes were looking right at me as I walked past. A shiver ran down my spine, but it wasn't from the cold. I shook my head and pushed the fear behind me. *It's just a doll; that's all it is, it's just a doll.* That's what I kept telling myself as I went into the kitchen. I used the small light above the stove to guide me, not wanting to wake Ethan with the light. I opened the fridge and found some pizza from two days ago, a perfect midnight snack. I grabbed the box and decided to take the whole thing up-stairs.

I turned around and started heading back. Ethan was still passed out, thankfully. I couldn't stop myself from looking at the doll. I shouldn't, I should just go upstairs and forget that it's there, but my eyes were drawn to it. I glanced at the chair and froze when the doll wasn't sit-ting in the spot anymore. I couldn't breathe; this was what I had feared the most. I didn't move, but my eyes roamed, trying to find the little thing. Luckily I didn't have to look too far, as it was lying on the ground by the chair leg, looking up, and still, somehow, its beady eyes were on me.

There was no plausible way the doll ended up like that on its own. It was sitting all the way against the back of the chair, and it could not have fallen to the floor. I took a shaky breath and continued back up the stairs. I wasn't going anywhere near the doll; no way in hell. I shut the door behind me, and just to be safe I even locked it. I let go of the breath I was holding and sat on the bed with the pizza box. It was warmer in the room, but I still couldn't stop shivering. I turned on the TV to add a bit of noise so it wasn't so silent. The nausea that was briefly forgotten in my terror hit back in full force.

I opened the box and took a big bite of the pepperoni pizza, hoping it would calm my stomach. I didn't realize how hungry I was until I started eating. It's surprising how hungry I was; I ate a large dinner at like 9:30, so I shouldn't be hungry already. I tried not to think about it as I ate with the cartoons playing in the background. I had eaten four slices, and the nausea hadn't gone away. I felt full, but still, the sick feeling stayed. I didn't feel like I would get sick, though; it was like I was stuck in limbo.

I sighed and sat back against the headboard, giving in to the idea that I was not getting any sleep. I watched the old cartoon on the TV, enjoying the nostalgia. I used to watch these cartoons as a kid; I loved that they still play them. I probably watched for another hour or so before I finally started to feel a bit sleepy. I was getting ready to move to lie down when I heard it.

I thought it was part of the cartoon, but it was coming from the hallway. A child's giggle sent another wave of shivers through me. I listened closely, letting the cartoon play, too scared of the silence. I strained my ears to listen past the cartoon, and for a moment, it was the only noise I could hear. Maybe I was just hearing things; it's late, and I'm tired and scared, so I could totally just be hearing things.

I sighed out a breath, and the sound came again, much closer. A child giggled just outside the bedroom door, followed by little footsteps running down the hall. I froze in place and stared at the door. I tried to think rationally, but there was nothing rational about it. So rather than rational, I tried to take the fear out of it. *This is just a child, that's all. They aren't going to hurt you; they aren't trying to scare you; it's a little kid. Maybe its spirit is happy to be in a home, perhaps it thinks it finally has a family, and that's why they're giggling; they're just exploring.*

While the idea satiated the fear, it made me a little sad. This spirit had been in that orphanage for so long, and now that we had their doll, they were able to go to a home. They're probably so happy, and I'm making Ethan take the doll back tomorrow; they'll have to go back to the orphanage. It hurt me a bit to think of it that way. I almost wanted to keep the doll just so I didn't hurt the poor thing. But it didn't belong to us, and it wouldn't be right. Besides, I wouldn't be able to get any sleep with the idea of there being a ghost in our house.

Feeling a little calmer about the situation, I was able to relax into my pillow. I still had the cartoons playing quietly in the background, but I felt I could get a bit of sleep now. I could still hear footsteps in the hall, and the sounds of the child giggling lingered, but I didn't let it bother me. I was almost asleep – just on the edge of consciousness – when I started shivering again. The room had grown as cold as it had been downstairs. I tucked the covers under my chin and wrapped my arms around myself, trying to warm up. I kept my eyes closed as I cuddled further into my bed, trying to shield myself from the frigid air.

It took all of five minutes before it was too cold for me. I was going to have to grab some blankets from the closet. I turned over and opened my eyes, getting ready to get up, when a shadow caught my eye. It was standing in the far corner of my room where the light from the TV didn't quite hit. The area was dark, but the shape was so much darker that I could see it clearly. It looked like a little girl standing there looking at me. I could see the silhouette of her hair hanging down her shoulders as it blew lightly from nonexistent wind. She only stood slightly over three feet tall, so she must have been young.

I tried not to let the shadow scare me, but the inherent fear still flowed through me. *It's just a child*; I reminded myself; *she's exploring, that's all.* I decided not to get up until she was gone; no matter how cold it was, I didn't want to disturb her. We sat there, seemingly just staring at each other. She didn't move or make any noise. Despite the cold, I started falling back to sleep because I was just lying there doing nothing.

"You took my doll." The whisper passed through my ears like she was right beside me, but she was still in the corner. The voice was so small, but it felt like a menacing creature was cornering me. I sucked in a breath, and my eyes shot open to stare at the figure again. She hadn't moved, but there was a different presence, it was intense, and it made my fight or flight instinct kick in, but I was stuck in freeze mode.

The room grew impossibly colder, my teeth started chattering and I could only curl into a ball. I couldn't look away from her, too scared she'd do something else. The only sound in the room now was the TV that had some- how turned into a blizzard; when did that happen? *It's just a child, it's just a child*, I kept repeating it to myself in my mind, but the reassurance wasn't there.

The sound of cracking and a deep groan filled the room, and my eyes nearly popped out of their sockets as the small figure of the girl moved for the first time. It bent and threw itself into positions that looked impossible and sounded painful. It kept moving and growing, taller and fuller. The limbs lengthened and reached out until the figure became fully grown. A stench forced its way into my nostrils, like that of rotting meat, and I nearly threw up everything in my stomach, fear being the only thing that stopped me.

"You stole my doll." The whisper was creaky and came out like a growl. My body shook, and a whimper escaped my throat before I could stop it. The sound was followed by a heavy footstep, then another. My heart nearly gave out as I watched the figure slowly make its way closer — another step, then another. *Do something, don't just sit there, do something!* She was so close, the rancid smell worsening as she got closer. "You will be punished." The growl was right in my ear. It was enough for my body to finally move and turn on the lamp next to my bed.

Once the light was on, everything stopped. The air in the room started warming back up, and the smell began to dissipate. My TV was back to normal, playing violent cartoons as if nothing had happened. My eyes flew around the room as I shuddered from the terror, but they found nothing. The clock read four in the morning.

The sun soon showed through the window. I hadn't moved from the spot I was in since I turned the light on. I just sat there for the last hour, quivering and waiting for that thing to come back. It never did, but I couldn't be too sure as it still made noises in the hallway. There were footsteps and something had been banging on the walls. I didn't have the guts to look. So, I sat there and waited for the sun.

It felt like I could breathe easier as the first light showed through my room; it was over, it was finally over. I had just breathed a sigh of relief when the doorknob started moving; someone was trying to come in. *No, you can't come out during the day like that; that's not how it's supposed to work!* I pulled my legs up to my chest as the knob continued to move. A loud bang on the door drew out the scream I had been holding in all night.

"Willow!" Ethan's voice sounded from the other side of the door, and the wave of relief that crashed through me sent me into tears. I jumped up from the bed and opened the door. "Why was the door locked- Hey! Will, what's wrong? What's going on?" I threw myself into his arms and cried into his chest. He held me tight and rubbed my hair. "Will, baby, what happened?" I tried to tell him, but I couldn't stop crying; I just continued to sob into his chest, and he held me until I was able to calm down. I felt him move his head to look past me. "What's that doing here?" I turned around, and the damned doll was on the floor, propped up against the leg of our bed.

I moved behind him, trying to hide from it. "Get it out, get that out of my house right now!" I kept yelling at him to get it out, and even though I could tell he was confused, he did as I said, grabbing the doll and taking it out into the car before coming back in.

"Willow, what is going on?" I was honestly surprised he didn't hear anything last night. I told him everything that happened, from the doll moving to the scary shadow. I had no idea how the thing even got into my room because I locked the door. "Will, no offense, but that sounds a little crazy." I almost started yelling, but he started talking again. "But you seem seriously terrified, so I feel like I gotta believe you." He pulled me into a hug again and rubbed my back. "They don't open until noon, so I'll take it back as soon as I can, okay." I sniffed and nodded in agreement.

Once the doll was out of the house, everything calmed down. I didn't feel like whatever was connected to it was still there. Ethan took it back to the orphanage, and I stayed home; I didn't want to be anywhere near that thing.

Ethan came back at around 12:30 with no doll in hand. "How'd it go?"

He shook his head and sat on the couch next to me. "I lied and told them my friend took it so I wouldn't get in trouble. I told them I took it from the friend to return it." I kicked him lightly for the lie but let him continue. "You're not gonna believe it, though. The lady was super shocked to see the doll. She said it's usually in storage and asked how my friend got it. I told her it was with the rest of the dolls when we were on the tour.

"Apparently, the doll doesn't actually belong to any of the kids, it belonged to the mean lady who killed all of them." He nodded to the shock on my face. "Yeah, they keep it in storage because people start acting weird when it's around. She told me, usually there are simple hauntings at the place like kids running around and giggling or playing, but when that doll is there, people get scratched, and they get sick, things get thrown around, and the lady said they see the form of something walking the halls that isn't a kid." I gave him a look that basically said that I told him so. "Yeah, I get it. I'm really sorry." He sounded genuinely sorry, which I was thankful for.

"Now we know never to steal things from haunted houses, right?"

"I will never steal anything from a haunted house again." He promised and held out his pinky for me to link.

"Good, and please, if we ever have kids, no dolls."

# NIGHTMARE

I was stuck. My back was glued to my bed, and my limbs felt like I had been drowned in anesthetic, except I was still aware of everything. I could still hear and see and smell. I tried to pull out of it, taking deep breaths to either relax my body into moving or help me drift back to sleep. It wasn't working; my heart began to thud in my chest with panic. *Okay, okay, I need to calm down; everything's fine.*

I moved my eyes around, thankful I could move something, and opened them. The panic that settled into my chest increased as I looked around my room. The curtains I had pulled shut were wide open, displaying the outside world illuminated by the moon. My closet door was cracked open and the door to the hall was completely ajar, even though they had both been closed when I went to sleep.

I tried to force my body to move and send those signals to my fingers, my toes, anywhere to get them moving, but nothing worked. I couldn't even make a noise, just stare around my room that had somehow moved on its own. My eyes darted around, feeling as though I was seeing things out of the corner of my eyes. I'd look one way and see a shadow moving to the left, and when I'd try look at it the shadow would move to the right. It was playing tricks on me, knowing I couldn't move to catch it. *No, it's not real; there is no shadow.*

Whispers reached my ears, crawling up the sides of my bed and tickling my eardrums. I couldn't understand what they were saying, but words were spoken from what felt like hundreds of voices, all overlapping to become indistinguishable. I wanted to scream at them to go away, but my voice was locked in my throat. "Here she is," "She's over here," "Come get her," the words became clearer as the voices became in sync.

The voices were soon accompanied by the scratching of the fabric next to my head. I couldn't turn to see what scurried over my sheets; I couldn't tell if the scratching was more related to a rat scurry or the claws of human hands. The hands played with me, I could see them in my mind: dozens of dirty, taloned hands reaching from under my bed, grasping for me and pulling at my sheets trying to pull themselves up to me. They pulled at the pillow, causing my head to shake slightly but never enough to turn it.

"She's here." The voices grew together in volume, calling to whoever was controlling them. Who were they calling? Who was looking for me? I stretched my ears, listening over the rustling of the sheets, waiting for the intruder. My eyes darted to the entrances to my room, waiting to see who would come in and devour me in my vulnerable state.

A croaking groan made its way into my room. It was like a cross between a woman and a frog trying to speak but were unable to. I tried to find the source, but it was like it was in both of my ears. My breathing quickened until I was almost hyperventilating. Something was coming for me, a thing I couldn't see or protect myself from.

I couldn't even jump when a bang hit my window. I stared wide-eyed, trying to find the source, but I couldn't see a hand or an object as one hit after the other shook the glass: *bang, Bang, BANG.* I couldn't even close my eyes out of fear of what would take advantage of the opportunity. Finally, the source came into view. A black hand landed against the window, the fingers were long, and the tips curved into talons. It felt like those fingers were scratching into my brain as they raked down the glass, causing it to screech.

The hand vanished from the window and the room became silent. The hands and voices disappeared from the bed, the groaning lady paused, and I was once again in my empty room. My breathing wouldn't calm down, and I still couldn't get my body to move. I was still stuck. I wanted to cry out and sob as I felt tears blur my eyes and leak over. I just wanted to fall back asleep and forget this ever happened.

The hinges of a door creaked their way into the hammering of my heart. I could barely see through the tears, so I couldn't see which door had moved. The creaking was joined with that sinister croaking woman, though it sounded more like a laugh this time. I blinked away the tears to figure out what was happening.

My room seemed to change with each blink. I could see better after the first; the closet door was slightly wider. The second brought a dark shadow cast over the wall from the closet. The third allowed that dark hand to return. It held onto the door, not moving it, just holding it; its hook-like fingers cast long shadows on the white paint, making it look rotten.

It slowly pushed, each creak of the old hinges like a sledgehammer strike on metal nails. *It's coming; it's coming to get me! I need to run; I need to get out of here. Move, damn it, you need to move!* My body refused to obey, only weeping more and blocking my vision from the horror of what-ever was about to enter my room. Through the tears, I could make out a charred arm, then a shoulder, and a leg followed, all lanky and burnt in color.

I didn't want to see it; I didn't want to watch as it came closer to hurt or eat me or whatever the hell demons do. I slammed my eyes shut as tight as I could in my paralyzed state. I refused to open them to see the thing move into the room. I could make out the sound of it pushing open the door and clambering its heavy feet closer and closer. The croaking from its throat felt like bugs crawling under my skin. It still didn't speak, just husked out its malign laugh, each wheeze assaulting my ears.

I could feel its breath over me; the decaying smell violated my nose, and I almost gagged, which would have been welcomed if it would allow me to move at all. Still, my body remained unmoving, allowing this thing to attack it. The grinding of teeth landed next to my ear; I could hear it licking its lips, looking at its meal and ready to consume. *GET UP, GET UP, MOVE, GET UP!* My mind raced as I tried to force myself free from whatever invisible chains I was captured in. If I could even move a finger, I could break free. My thoughts pushed and pushed, trying to force me to get away from the mouth in my face, but it was to no avail. I was trapped; I was going to die.

With the thought, everything stopped. The mouth and accompanying noises disappeared; no more creaking and groaning, the only sound was the wind outside. Was it gone? Should I look? Something deep in me told me not to, to keep my eyes shut until the sun came up. But another part of me told me to check to make sure; I needed to see to ensure it was gone. Slowly, I let my eyes crack open.

I was met with the face that would haunt my night-mares for the rest of my life. She had no eyes, her dark rotting mouth hung open in a silent scream, and her lanky starved body looked as though it had been burnt to a char, but her hair hung wet around her face, caging me in as she hung over me. I couldn't scream though every inch of my body was ready to run away shrieking bloody murder. Though, my muscles didn't agree. I knew then I would die without a fight from this monster, this demon, who would devour my insides as I watched in incapaci-tated fear.

I could hear her laughing throughout my head as tears drenched my face silently, waiting, choking on my breath; I was surprised my heart hadn't already given out from the fright of it all. I prayed to let it be quick, to let it be over soon; I prayed that I wouldn't suffer, though the howling from above me ensured that suffering was not optional.

I found the nerve to close my eyes again; I couldn't bear to watch what she would do to me. I sent a silent message to my family that they'll never get and a final prayer as I awaited my end.

"Mommy?" My son's voice rang over the howling in my head and silenced the rest of the noise. In that second, I felt like the chains holding me down vanished, and I could finally move. My body shot up, and I was glad I didn't knock into the monster that had loomed over me only seconds ago. I gasped as though I hadn't taken a breath in hours and looked at my room. The curtains were shut, as was the closet door. There was no sign of anyone else in the room besides my young son standing at the bedroom door with his little elephant. He looked scared as he stood there. "Mommy, I had a bad dream. Can I sleep in here with you?"

A sigh left me, and I was finally able to wipe the tears from my cheeks, "Yeah, baby, you can sleep in here." I sniffed, and he ran to join me.

We settled back into the bed, but I couldn't relax or fall back to sleep just yet. "Did you have a bad dream, too?" I looked down at my baby, his little face calming me and bringing me back to reality.

"Yeah, baby, just a bad dream. Let's go back to sleep."

# A 3

The last box fell out of my hands. "Is that it?" Bailey asked, leaning against the little peninsula separating the kitchen from my new apartment's living room.

With a massive sigh of relief, I confirmed her question. "I think so." I had grabbed the last box from the van and there wasn't anything else I had left back home. "Thanks again, sis; I couldn't have done it without you." I went over and messed up her hair like I knew she hated, but what kind of brother would I be if I didn't mess with her all the time?

"Yeah, I know." She pushed my hand away and fixed her golden hair back into place. I was really going to miss having her around every day, but growing up and getting my first place was far more important.

"Kenny," my best friend called from my new bathroom, "where's the toilet paper?"

I chuckled and shook my head. "It's under the sink!" I yelled back. I looked around my new space and bit my lip anxiously. Almost every surface had a bag or box covering it, and it was about to get dark. I didn't need them driving the half an hour it took for them to get back to their own homes at night. "If you wanna head home, I can take it from here," I told my sister as I ran my hand through my hair. She was still living at home with our parents and I didn't need them worrying about where she was.

She shook her head, "Nah, I'll help you unpack a bit then crash on your couch. I'll even go pick up some pizza because I'm just the nicest sister anyone could ask for." She stated in a sarcastic tone, but she really is. She didn't have to help me move all my shit and help me unpack it all.

"Pizza?" Luke's head peaked out from the hallway. "Did I hear you say pizza?" He wiped his hand down his bearded chin. He was always looking for food; when we were in high school, he brought snacks to all our classes and still had a big lunch. I never knew where he put it all, considering he was still skinny as a twig.

"Yeah, I'm buying. What do you want?" Bailey took out her phone and opened the website to order the pizza.

"Bacon, sausage, and peppers. Extra cheese, too." He sat on the ugly, brown, hand-me-down couch I got from my parents, spreading his arms over the back and putting his feet on the table. At least someone feels at home already.

She rolled her eyes and turned to me. "Pepperoni for you?" She asked.

"Yes, please." I smiled, thankful for her kindness.

She nodded and headed towards the door. "I'll be back in thirty. Don't do anything stupid." With that, she shut the door behind her.

"Your sister's so hot, dude," Luke said from the couch. I scoffed and hit him on the back of his head, making him wince. He was constantly trying to get my sister's attention, no matter how many times she turned him down or I threatened him to leave her be.

"And too good for you," I added before grabbing the first box in the open kitchen. "Why do you even keep trying? That's like the ultimate rule in the bro code. Don't date your best friend's sister." I shivered in disgust at the idea of those two actually having a relationship. I began stacking the dishes in the cabinets and putting away the utensils.

"Yeah, but as my best friend, you should still be trying to help me." I could hear the smirk in his voice, even if I couldn't see him.

I moved around the corner to glare at him. "You're not dating my sister," I said sternly and waited for him to rebuttal. But he never did, thankfully. He just groaned and started picking through the boxes. We grew silent after that, pulling stuff from boxes and placing them where they belonged. Bailey returned a while later with three pizza boxes, and we took a break.

As we ate, Luke walked around the living room and spied through some of the windows. "You know you can see right through the neighbor's window, right?" He spoke around the pizza in his mouth. "Maybe there's a super-hot chick that leaves her curtains open at night." He chuckled at his own joke; I only shook my head.

"Only you would let that be your first thought, you perv." I took another big bite of my pizza and rolled my eyes. My first thought was that I hoped there wasn't a grandma that liked to walk around in the nude. I did not need that to scar me for the rest of my life.

"Come on, dude, you're twenty-three years old, you can't tell me you haven't thought about the possibility of meeting some hot chick you watch change from the window. That's some sexy foreplay right there." He moved his hips provocatively, and my sister and I both made disgusted noises at him.

"This is why you'll never get a girlfriend." Bailey chimed in. The sad puppy look on his face made both of us laugh.

The sound of an upbeat pop song broke through the room. Bailey reached for her phone and answered it. "Hello?" Her features became concerned as she listened to the voice on the other side. I couldn't make out the words, but someone was yelling or crying. "Okay, okay, calm down; it's not the end of the world. I can come get you. I'll be there in a few." She hung up and grabbed her stuff. "Sorry, Kenny, Ariana needs help getting home. Her car broke down, and she's freaking out about it. I'm gonna go get her and take her home. I'll come back to-morrow and help some more." She waited for me to respond before dashing out the door.

"No problem, Bails, I got it." I got up from the couch and gave her a quick hug. "Be careful, okay? It's getting late."

"I'll be fine. See ya, bro." I watched as she walked out before returning to my spot on the couch. There were a few more slices left, but I was getting full. I closed the box and took it and Bailey's pizza to the fridge. I'll just save it for tomorrow for breakfast or lunch.

The sound of Luke wiping his hands together brought my attention back to him. "I'm gonna have to leave soon, too, man. I told Nat I'd be home by ten and it'll take me an hour to get there. They've got the freaking road blocked, so I have to go the long way around." He shoved the last of his concoction of a pizza in his mouth. He never ceases to amaze me with how much he can eat.

"No problem, man. I'll probably just wait to finish up tomorrow." I grabbed a bottle of water from the fridge and took a long drink as he threw his pizza box in the trash. "I'm dead tired, so once you leave, I'll probably just hit the sack."

"Sure, man. I'll get out of your hair. I got work tomorrow, so I'll probably see you this weekend?" He asked as he pulled on his shoes.

"Works for me," I replied and took another drink. He gave me a quick hug before grabbing his things and leaving.

I sighed and looked around my now empty apartment. Since it was quiet, I could hear the neighbors moving around above and below me. I finished my water and headed to my room. It was a little smaller than my old one back home, but I could still fit a queen-sized bed and a dresser and still have some walking room. I pulled my shirt off and sat on the bed to look out the window. There wasn't much of a view; there was another apartment building only about ten feet from mine. As Luke said, I could see into the room across from me.

I was getting ready to go to bed when movement caught my eye. I looked up to see a figure standing in the window facing mine. A woman with long black hair was looking through my window. She looked about my age, with pale skin under her tank top, and I could make out the blue in her eyes. A smile grew on her face when she saw me looking at her. I gave a little embarrassed smile back. She waved at me with a small hand before walking in another direction. She returned moments later with a notepad and marker in her hands. My brow furrowed in confusion. Was she really trying to talk to me with a pen and paper? Why not just talk to me? Then I thought maybe she couldn't speak or hear or just likes to be quirky. Either way, she was cute, so I didn't really care. She flipped her pad of paper around, and the words, *Hi, I'm Melanie*, were written in pretty handwriting.

I smiled and held up my finger to tell her to hold on a second. I ran into my living room to find the box that held my office supplies. Luckily, it wasn't buried under a ton of stuff. I grabbed a marker and a large paper pad and returned to my room. She was still sitting there, waiting for me. *Hello, I'm Kenny.*

Her smile widened when I answered her. *Nice to meet you. Just move in?* She answered.

I chuckled and wrote out my reply. *Yeah, today. Have you been here long?*

*A few years. It's nice.* She grinned throughout our little interaction, and I couldn't help but smile back.

*I'm liking it so far.* I could make out a slight blush on her cheeks as she read my response.

*Would you want to come over and meet the neighbor?* She bit her lip as I read it, her head cocked slightly, letting her hair fall over her face.

It was my turn to blush at her boldness. *Sure, when?*

*Now?* I watched her shrug her shoulders as I read it. I thought for a second, would it really be a good idea to go over to her house this late? I looked back over at her and saw her smile again. It really made her face glow, there weren't any wrinkles on her clear skin, and I wanted to feel how smooth it was. Yep, I'll go.

I nodded to her and asked for her apartment number.

*A3!* She grinned and hopped a bit in place when she answered. I chuckled and held up my finger again to tell her I'll be there in a minute.

I threw my shirt back on and fixed my hair with my hand. I grabbed my phone and keys and quickly headed to the building next door. *I can't believe I'm actually doing this,* I thought. I was going over to a complete stranger's place just because I thought they were cute. But this is what being an adult is: meeting new people, finding love, and having fun. Who cares that it's late? I was going to meet this cute neighbor and see where things go. The front door was unlocked and I jogged up the stairs to the apartment number she gave me. The three flights of stairs seemed like nothing as I stood before her door.

I took a deep breath and lifted my hand to knock, but the door opened before my hand could touch it. I smiled, expecting to see her beautiful face on the other side of the door, but it quickly faded when all I saw was a dark, empty room. I looked around the landing, thinking I got the wrong floor, but the door clearly stated 'A3.' I stepped into the doorway, hoping to see her around the corner, that it was just a fun little joke on the new neighbor.

I couldn't see her anywhere. It didn't look like anyone had lived there in a while. The little bit of furniture in the room had white sheets over them, and everything was covered in dust. There was no way this was the right place. This was just a cruel joke. I scoffed and turned to leave but the door shut in front of me, blocking my way out. My heartbeat quickened as I pulled at the door handle to no avail. I twisted the knob and pulled with all my strength, but the door was not opening.

I felt something grab my shoulder, and I froze. I looked down to see a petite hand with pink polish. I sighed in relief and turned quickly to see the girl, Melanie, grinning at me. She wore a white nightgown now instead of the tank top and shorts, but there were red stains all over it. Did she get hurt? I was about to voice my concern when she spoke. "I'm so happy you came. My husband won't be home for a while." Husband? What the hell? But there was something strange about her voice. It was like three voices were overlapping as she spoke.

She moved closer into my space until our chests were inches away. The room grew colder, and I shook. I could see my shaky breath leave my mouth. "Why are you living in a place like this? And what do you mean, husband?" My voice shook slightly from the cold; I felt like I walked into a freezer.

"Don't worry, darling; you don't have to worry about him." Her smile became creepier by the second, curling wider as she spoke. Her hands slid up my chest and snaked around my shoulder. They stung like a block of ice, but I couldn't pull away. "I love getting visitors," her tone turned dark, and the echo of a large crowd sounded as she spoke. She stood on her toes and leaned closer until I felt her lips brush against mine. They were frozen, and I could only close my eyes and shiver.

Just as quickly as she was there, I opened my eyes and she was gone. I looked around and released the breath I didn't realize I was holding. She disappeared! Like vanished! *I need to get out of here.* I grabbed at the door handle and yanked at it, but it was stuck in place. I started banging on it, hoping one of the neighbors would hear it and come to my rescue.

A strange sound came from down the hall, like a storm's wind. It froze me in place. The sense of dread, of death, flooded through me as I turned back to the apartment. I looked up in time to see Melanie, but she was wrong. She was no longer the beautiful temptress that lured me into this trap; she was a monster. Her throat was slashed, dark blood pouring from her neck down her clothes. Her face looked bludgeoned and broken; her jaw hung open, and the side of her head looked scalped. I didn't even have time to scream as she let out a terrifying wail and lunged at me. Daggered claws and bloodied eyes were the last things I saw before my world exploded into pain, then nothing.

# THE WELL

Their mother tells them that the woods aren't safe to play in, but Holly thinks she's just worried they'll get lost. Felix and Holly love playing in the woods. It always smells nice, and they get to see beautiful animals all the time. They never go too far because then they would get in trouble. Their mother always makes sure they can hear her as they play, and if they don't answer her when she calls, they aren't allowed outside the next day.

Felix loves to collect the leaves that fall from the trees and the wildflowers that grow beautifully in the Spring. He puts them in a book to hold onto them forever. His mother showed him how to make sure they never grow brown. At ten years old, he has already decided he wants to work with plants as an adult. He wants to grow as many flowers and trees as possible and cover the world with them.

Holly, on the other hand, found the odd parts of the woods more fascinating. Where Felix adored the beauty, Holly admired the pieces often shunned by society. The tiny rabbit bone she found under a bush sits in a little jar on her nightstand. The deceased crow she had crossed paths with offered her beautiful black feathers she uses as bookmarks. Don't worry; she cleaned them. Her mother is sure she will grow up to work with the dead; no ten-year-old should be so enthralled by bones and corpses. But Holly says she wants to work with animals.

Spring this year has brought many new things to their isolated haven. A hungry mastiff found his way to their cabin; where he came from, they weren't sure, as the closest town was five miles away. But they feed and care for him; he now sleeps in the children's room, usually cuddled up to Holly. He has become an excellent farm hand, rounding up the sheep and the few cattle they own. They have to keep him away from the chickens, though; he finds them quite tasty.

He doesn't like to follow them into the woods, which the children find strange. This is the best area to run around and play! There are so many sticks to play fetch with; even a few deer bones are scattered around if you know where to look. Alas, Monty – the name the children gave him – sits at the forest's edge watching them play but never crosses the tree line.

Holly has found that there are quite a few more bones this year. As she scours their play area, she's surprised by the things she finds. The first warm day of the season drew them to the green forest. It's quieter than usual, but maybe the animals are still waking from their long winter sleep. She runs through the trees, and Felix chases her in a game of tag; Monty sits on the outside, watching closely. She rounds a bush and stops in her tracks, allowing Felix to slap his hand on her shoulder. It causes no reaction, though, as she's too intrigued by the nearly complete skeleton of a raccoon.

The skull is intact, but the rest of the bones were tossed into a pile under the shrubbery. Where did this come from? What kind of animal could have possibly eaten the little thing so carefully as to pile the bones together right after consumption? It reminds Holly of how her father eats chicken wings, the bones tossed onto a plate after the meat had been devoured. As she looks closer, she sees teeth markings on the bones but can't place what kind of animal they belong to.

Felix blanches, looking at the corpse; he never understood his twin's love for dead things. Where was the beauty in it? Death isn't supposed to be beautiful; it's sad and rotten. The skeleton at their feet proves his point. Why does Holly insist on collecting such horrible things? Is she not scared? The bones lying here mean a larger, hungrier creature is lurking around, ready to snag them, too. The idea sends a shiver down Felix's spine, and he scopes the woods. They seem darker in the daylight; ominous shadows sway in the distance, waiting to pounce on them. "We should go; whatever ate that thing could still be out here." He warns his sister.

She crouches on the ground, collecting the bones she wants to take home. She looks up at him with a pout. "What do you mean? I'm sure we're fine." She brushes off the warning and continues leafing through the bones. She isn't afraid like her brother. He's always been weirded out by her hobbies; he's just a little scaredy cat.

"Come on, Holly; it could be a mountain lion or a wolf!" He urges on and pulls at her shirt.

"Well, it already ate, so it won't be hungry if it comes back." Felix is flabbergasted by her logic. She's willing to sit out here as lion meat for a couple of bones?

"I'll tell Mom." He threatens, finally drawing serious attention from Holly. She glares at him and stands, the bones tucked into the little pocket she made with her shirt. She huffs, and Felix pulls her out of the trees to meet Monty. He sits in the sun, panting lightly, but he seems as relaxed as he is in front of the fireplace. "Let's go, Monty." Felix orders and Monty follows. He sniffs Holly's shirt briefly before she pushes his face away. These are her bones, not his.

The season continues the same. The children go out to play, Monty close behind, and then Felix gets scared by something as he collects his leaves and flowers. They see many things that are not of the ordinary. The crows have grown in numbers as the weather grows warmer, and they all sit and watch the children as they play. Holly believes them to be their friends, as Felix remembers what a group of crows is called. Animal bones continue to pop up, and Holly's naïve mind can't seem to find a place for any fear like her brother.

"I don't want to go play," Felix states. The warm June day offers the perfect weather to run around outside. The months of fear have finally reached their limits, and Felix is scared of what they might find if they continue to go out into the woods. "Let's stay inside today." He offers a compromise.

Holly rolls her eyes; her brother is such a scaredy cat. "You can stay inside; I'm going to look for treasure!" She exclaims and runs out of the house without another word, Monty following. She enjoys the warm sun on the walk to the tree's edge. The cows graze on the far end of the farm, and she can hear the sheep bleating from their pen. How could Felix say staying inside is a better idea? It's so beautiful outside; the birds sing from their perches in the trees and draw Holly closer to them.

Monty takes his position as a guard dog as she enters, though he does not relax in his usual seat. Holly doesn't mind her dog; instead, she looks around for more treasures. She has collected many bones recently; maybe she can find some feathers or an abandoned nest. She explores the ground and the trees, digs into the bushes, and looks under fallen logs, but she can't find anything interesting. But she doesn't give up; she plans on returning home with a new and fantastic treasure today, and that's what she'll do!

She travels further into the trees; the canopy covers the sun and darkens the forest floor. Monty whines from the outside and paces the boundary but doesn't follow. Holly jumps over a mound of boulders and disappears from his sight. His barking falls deaf on her ears as she ventures deeper, the excitement of the exploration wiping her memory of any and all warnings from her mother about going too deep into the woods.

A small crow lands at her feet and cocks his head as if confused by her appearance. He caws at her before flying off to the left. The interaction makes Holly laugh, and she follows him. She chases him past more trees and odd-shaped rock formations. Her giggling echoes through the greenery. She finally finds him again as he perches on the edge of a small brick wall. A brick wall? What is something like this doing in the middle of the woods?

Holly moves closer to inspect the wall and finds it is rounded with a deep hole in the center. "A well?" She mutters out loud in wonder. She's lived here her whole life and never knew of a well in the woods. The stones were aged, with vines and moss growing over them. The smell of musk and damp earth seeps into the air around it. Holly circled the well, investigating the exterior. It does not unsettle her to see claw marks and specks of blood on the old stone. It is a forest, after all, maybe a small animal was exploring as she is.

A noise surprises her. It's not like any animal she's ever heard before. The sound is low and guttural, a moan of pain or hunger. But where is it coming from? She looks around the forest, but the only animal in sight is the little crow that led her there. The noise continues, drawing her attention back to the well. Her heart sinks; a poor animal has fallen in and is now hurt, dying a slow, painful death. Her heart breaks a little. While she likes to collect the bones of dead animals, the act of dying still hurts her soul.

She looks over the edge, trying to see if she can help. Maybe if it's not too deep, she can grab some rope and help the poor thing. The hole is dark, too dark to see anything clearly. The loss of sunlight from the trees didn't help either. "It's okay, I'm gonna get you out." She yells down, trying to comfort the mystery creature. The echo that bounces back gives light to the depth of the well. But Holly is too ambitious; she is going to help this animal. She just has to be able to see it to get it.

She leans over further, bent at the stomach, her head ducking past the top layer of brick. The moaning sound gets closer. It's closer than she thought! She can reach down and grab it and pull it to safety. She steadies herself on the brick and reaches her hand down as far as she can go. She teeters, just barely balancing, as she tries to feel for the hurt animal. It brushes something. Just a bit further! There it is again, just need to grab it.

Something wraps around her wrist, and she loses her balance, not even able to scream as the darkness closes around her. In the distance, Monty howls into the forest; Felix and his mother run to him and call for Holly. They search for her as far as they can go, and a crow watches them from the trees.

# BLACK-EYED

The long-used phrase "the eyes are the windows to the soul" isn't just words of poetry but also words of warning. You see so much in the eyes of another person: their feelings, their thoughts, their pasts, their present, and their future. A person's entire story can be told through those tiny but complex organs. And you can keep yourself safe by reading that story. I think it goes without saying, though, that if you encounter someone whose eyes reflex the blackness of their soul, you run as far as you can.

There have been many tales of black-eyed children. You've heard of children in the corn and changelings, but none of them are as creepy as the black-eyed children. There are many stories behind what black-eyed children truly are. Some say they are the ghosts of children who were abandoned or killed by their parents, looking for someone to take them home or shelter them. Some say they are clay-like creatures created by a demon or monster to lure innocent, helpful victims into their lair. Others say they themselves are the monsters seeking the flesh of those foolish enough to fall into their claws.

Either way, in all tales, the most important thing to remember is never to let them in. They are all soulless creatures, after all. Some have listened to this warning; others have ignored it.

Lyla sat waiting in her car for her husband to leave the store. They had just come from the doctors, seeing a four-month ultrasound of the newest member of their family. They still aren't sure what the gender is, and the excitement of getting to shop for tiny clothes and shoes is all she could think about. After the appointment, she had mentioned wanting to bake later today, so her husband Ray drove to the nearest grocery store. She was going to go in with him, but he insisted that she stay in the car and not over-exert herself.

He has been so protective of her and the baby. Sometimes it went a bit too far, but it was sweet how much he cared for her. The house was always clean, and he made her whatever she wanted. He gave her massages and brought home all the little things she craved. She was so excited to see him be a father; he had always wanted to be. She didn't argue when he insisted she'd stay in the car, knowing he knew exactly what she needed and honestly too tired to want to walk around more. The appointment was so early, so she was going to go back to the house, nap, and then bake.

There was a knock on the door which had her opening her eyes. She looked out her window to find two small children, a boy and a girl no more than twelve years old. The boy had an old baseball cap covering short black hair, and the girl had long curly blonde hair and bangs. Both of their clothes were tattered, and their skin was dirty.

Lyla sat up quickly and opened the window. The poor little things, they're probably homeless and hungry. "Hello, miss, could you help us? We're lost and can't get back home. Could you help us get back home?" The little girl spoke, her voice rasped from thirst.

Lyla's heart sank, and in her over-emotional state felt herself start to tear up. "Oh, you poor kids, of course. My husband is in the store; we can give you a ride home once he comes out, okay?" She smiled sweetly at the little darling, her maternal instincts screaming at her to care for these kids. She should call Ray and have him get something for them to eat; they look starving. "Are you hungry? I can call him to grab you some food. Why don't you sit in the car until he comes back?" She unlocked the doors, and the children, oddly stiffly, climbed into the back seat.

"Oh, thank you. We're so hungry." The little boy answered.

She nodded back to them and pulled out her phone. He answered after the first ring. "Hello, my love. Is everything okay?"

She smiled at the greeting. "Yes, um, Ray, there were these two little children; they're lost and look like they haven't eaten in days. Could you grab something for them to eat; I said we could take them home. I don't know how far yet. But I couldn't bare to leave them on the street." She practically begged, peaking back at the children.

She could hear him smile through the phone. "Of

course, baby, I was just finishing up, but I'll grab some deli sandwiches and water and be out soon. I love you."

She gave him her love back and hung up, turning back to the children. They sat stiffly in the seat, mirroring each other as they sat back straight, legs together, and hands folded on their laps. They looked straight forward until she turned to them, then they faced her in unison. "My husband will be out in a few minutes. Where is your home? Do you remember the address?" She opened the GPS on her phone, ready to punch it in. The girl gave her an address, "This is two counties over. How did you end up over here?"

"We were staying with a family member, and they were not nice to us, so we ran away." The girl responded. Lyla's heart broke seeing the darkened spots on their skin, now looking more like bruises than dirt. "You are very kind to help us."

That motherly feeling returned, "What kind of person would let two children stay on the streets? I'm a mother, and if my child ever got into a situation like that, I would go crazy. I'm sure your parents are so worried."

"Oh, you have a child?" The boy asked. There was something in the way he asked that sent ice down Lyla's spine. Suddenly the maternal feeling towards these children had turned to dread. Where was this feeling coming from? Why was she so frightened?

"Y-yes, well, I'm actually carrying my baby right now in my belly." She tried to keep that warm, motherly voice, but the dread wouldn't go away. She felt trapped in the car like prey being stalked and captured by some horrific predator.

"Wow, that baby is going to have a good mom." The boy responded and looked up from under his cap. The ice running down her spine burned. "I wish we had a mom like you." He continued, and she watched the girl nod beside him, her bangs bouncing away from her eyes. Lyla's body ran cold, and her muscles tensed as she gazed into the two pairs of blackened eyes staring back at her.

She gulped down the bile that began to rise in her throat. "That's very nice." It came out as a whisper as fear wrapped around her body, a hungry snake constricting its way through her limbs. She had to run and hide; she needed to get away from these children. She cleared her throat. "I'm going to go check on Ray." She spat out before rushing out of the car and running into the store, not looking back at the things in her car.

Once safely inside, she leaned against the closest wall and caught her breath, ignoring the odd stares she was getting. "Lyla?" Ray's concerned voice broke through her panic, and she burst into tears as she felt his familiar arms run around her. "Sweetie, what happened? Are you hurt?" She felt his hands check over her, rubbing over her slightly protruding stomach before grabbing her face. "Lyla, what happened? Where are those kids?" The mention of the kids brought out another sob.

It took a while for her to calm down. They stood there near the store entrance, Ray comforting his hysterical pregnant wife, so confused as to what could have upset her. After another five minutes, she was able to breathe again, the dreadful feeling had dissipated, but the fear stuck. "Lyla, please tell me what's wrong. Did someone hurt you? Did something happen to the kids?"

She sobbed again but didn't let it get further than that. She couldn't stop shaking her head, thinking back to those empty eyes inside the innocent-looking faces of those children. "Those weren't kids, Ray; they were something else." She paused to catch her breath. She could see Ray's confused face through the blur of her tears. "Their eyes. They weren't... they were all black like they weren't even there."

Ray, still confused, rubbed the tears from his wife's face, letting her tell her story. It was odd, but even in her hormonal state, there was no way she would be freaking out like this without reason. It made it hard not to believe her. Though he always thought those things were myths, black-eyed children were made-up stories.

Once he was able to calm down his wife, he grabbed the bags and escorted her out of the store and back to their car. She became more hesitant as they got closer. Her body shook in his arms when the little green car came into view. He let go of her waist and walked ahead slightly to check it out. The car was still running; looking through the back window, he couldn't see anyone inside. The only thing wrong with the car was that the rear passenger door was left ajar.

He quickly gathered their bags and his wife into the car and drove off. He had a feeling she wouldn't go out alone for a while, which he was completely okay with. Her hand was clamped around his own, still shaking slightly but calming down more the closer they got to the house. He decided not to mention the two children on the side of the road, a girl with blonde hair and a boy with a baseball cap, staring at the car as it drove out of the parking lot.

# GHOST TOWN

"How much further?" Dorothy whined from the back seat. We've been on the road for almost eight hours now, and to my knowledge, we had about ten more to go until we reached Vegas. I was glad we stopped for gas at the last town because we were in the middle of absolutely nowhere. If someone had told me that driving from Austin to Vegas would be a dreadful idea, I might have spared the cash for a flight ticket.

We just passed the Arizona state line not too long ago and are now driving through the dry-ass desert. I was a little thankful we chose to make this trip now in June rather than August like we originally planned, it hadn't reached the deathly-hot stage yet, but the temperature still sucks at a nearly melting 90 degrees. The mountains at least gave us a pretty view to drive through; Angie's camera clicked nonstop.

"We've got about ten more hours. We'll hit Phoenix in about three or four." I informed her, looking at the MapQuest directions. I figured it was easier to print them out just in case our phones died or we lost service. "We'll be on this road for a while." I sighed, mostly to myself.

The air was blasting, and the music thrummed through the otherwise silent car. Antonio was napping in the backseat, Dorothy had her headphones in, and Angie was looking out the windows. It was a peaceful ride. There weren't many other cars on the road even though it was seven in the evening; I guess we were just on a stretch of road that didn't get much traffic. The only other vehicles we saw were primarily semitrucks.

I relaxed in my seat the more I drove, enjoying the views and the ride. These were the types of drives I loved the most, where you could just go without having to worry about anyone else on the road, without idiots or crashes to keep an eye out for. I sighed in contentment and let a small smile slip onto my face.

"Oooh, look, that sign says there's a ghost town up there." Angie pointed out an old road sign. It was a town sign, but it faded with age so I couldn't quite read the name of the town. There was another, newer sign above it that stated: "ABANDONED KEEP OUT." I simply hummed in acknowledgment and started to let it slip from my mind. "We should go check it out." She turned to me in excitement.

"Can you not read? It said to keep out." I scolded her and shook my head.

She grabbed my arm and shook it slightly. "Come on, Krys, let's just go take a peak; it'll probably look super cool. Plus, I would love to take some pictures." She pouted, her puppy dog look complete with her dark brown eyes.

"What is she whining about?" Dorothy asked with one of her earbuds in her hand.

"There's a ghost town a few miles up, and I wanna go check it out, but Krys won't let me." She whined. I looked in the rearview mirror to see Antonio had woken up from the noise and was looking at her with tired eyes.

"The sign said to keep out. I'm not trying to get arrested or killed just so you can take pictures." I rolled my eyes and looked back at the road.

"She's right, Ang; it might not be safe if they want people to stay out." Antonio agreed, his voice a little husky from sleep.

"I think it would be fun." Dorothy had a wicked smile as she took out her other earbud. "What's the matter, you guys too chicken?" She teased and elbowed Antonio playfully.

I huffed and shook my head. "I'm not scared, I'm just trying to keep everyone safe. There could be someone there who shoots intruders. Did you think about that? Plus, we have to get to the hotel." I tightened my grip on the steering wheel and looked back at the road.

"I highly doubt that. It says abandoned, meaning no one is there." Angie egged on and giggled. "Please, Krys, just for a little. We don't need to be at the hotel until tomorrow; we have plenty of time. Hell, we're going to be so early that we won't be able to check in yet because of your OCD ass. We can take a few minutes detour." I looked at her to see her batting her eyelashes at me.

The two girls badgered me together, and Antonio was no longer any help. "Fine!" I groaned and shook my head. "We will go for a few minutes, and that's it. But if we see anyone or if it's blocked off, we leave. Got it?" They both whooped and clapped as they celebrated, which only hurt my head. "Where the hell am I going?" I grumbled to Angie, and she pointed in the direction the sign said.

From the main road, you could barely see the formations of a town that I assumed was in the direction we were heading. There was a road to turn down that went toward the site, and I followed it. The girls looked out the windows in excitement as we got closer. The town was about ten minutes from the main road, but it was just a straight road to go down.

The closer we got, the better I could see. There wasn't any fence or blockage to keep people out, which I thought was weird, especially when the sign specifically said to keep out. It was an old western town, like the ones you see in old cowboy movies. The road led into the town center, and buildings branched off for about a mile in each direction. There weren't any cars that I could see, so maybe there wasn't anyone there.

I stopped the car in what probably used to be the very center of town as the road opened into a large circle. "We can look around for a few minutes and then leave, got it?" The rest of the passengers were looking out the windows in awe and didn't answer right away. "Got it?" I asked louder, and they snapped their heads at me. "Don't stray too far."

They nodded and eagerly got out of the car, even Antonio, who had initially been against coming down here. I followed suit and closed the door behind me. The first thing I noticed was how quiet it was. There weren't any people or cars bustling around and causing traffic. The wind blew through the empty buildings causing a few old doors to sway lightly on their rusted hinges. Not even a desert bird flew overhead.

I looked around the center and took in the town; the buildings were still surprisingly well put together, the wood was breaking apart a bit, and all the signs were worn to nothing, but it wasn't in ruins. I wondered how long this place had been abandoned. Had it been a hundred years or only a decade? Why did it become a ghost town? I'd always wondered that when someone talked about ghost towns. How did it become a ghost town? Why would everyone abandon a perfectly good town? I understand that in some cases, it's because resources ran out, but there are some that seemingly just die overnight.

My friends had gone off on their own to look around, so I was stuck exploring by myself. The evening sun was hot, and the lack of shade wasn't helping as I walked down the road. I peeked into the buildings as I went. They mostly looked like old businesses, as many had old counters and shelves that were all empty. There were two buildings opposite each other in the circle. I walked over to one and went through the large wooden doors.

They led into a large room filled with desks and bookshelves. The old classroom still had a few of its accessories. Stacks of books sat around on the bookshelves, and little toys were huddled in the far corner.

There were still streaks of chalk on the green board in the front of the room. I walked over to the teacher's desk and found a few old pieces of paper that were no longer readable and a couple of tools like a ruler and a few pencils.

I could almost picture the schoolhouse filled with the town's children, their smiling faces learning and playing. The glass in the windows was either gone or broken, and the dust from the outside covered everything. It made the room darker and eerie. I walked around the room and took in as much as I could. I could make out faded markings on the little desks and ran my fingers over them, feeling the indentations. I chuckled lightly, picturing a little girl carving the name of her crush into the desk and getting in trouble for it.

I heard a giggling sound and looked around. It sounded close like it was in the room with me, but it must have been the wind carrying Angie's or Dorothy's voice. I moved over to the bookshelves and pulled out the books that were there. I found some familiar titles that had changed through the years, a few notebooks with children's handwriting, and a couple of old textbooks. I smiled at the discovery. A tug on the back of my shirt had me whirling around. It was like a little hand had pulled on it to get my attention, but there wasn't anyone there. There wasn't anything I could see that would cause the movement either.

I stood up quickly and walked out of the building and back into the center. I could faintly hear Angie and Dorothy laughing in the distance. I sighed; I told them not to go too far. Not that it would be hard to call them back.

I looked across the street to the other building; this one was slightly bigger and more official. I walked over and tested the saloon-style doors before pushing them open with a loud creak. There was a large desk on the right as I entered, and on the left was a row of cells; some of their doors hung open. There was another door in front of me, and I could slightly make out the word "SHERIFF" written across it. There was a strange smell: slightly musty but a little rotten, probably from the old wood and the rust on the metal bars. A strange shiver ran over me, and I got the feeling that I shouldn't be here like someone was watching me. I shook it off, feeling ridiculous for the paranoia.

I pushed open the door and went into the sheriff's office. I was surprised to find it still in its original condition. The shelves were lined with old books, and the desk was covered in stuff. I saw papers, some keys, and some other things I couldn't quite figure out. I pushed around some items, trying to see if I could read some of the papers; most were just smudgy ink, and some were legible but didn't make much sense.

I pulled one of the books from the shelf, coughing a bit from the cloud of dust that popped out when I dropped it on the desk. There weren't any words on the front, but when I opened it, I could tell it was a ledger of some sort. I flipped through the pages, not really reading, just looking. A creak could be heard from the outside of the room. It sounded like the front door opening; *I guess the rest of them found their way here.*

"I'm back here," I called to them and waited. When

no one responded, I looked out the door. I didn't see any-one at the main entrance or hear anyone walking around. I shrugged and looked back at the book, thinking it was just the old wood moving under the unfamiliar weight. I flipped another page and fell into the back wall hearing the loud clang of metal against metal. I ran into the lobby, still finding no one, but the open cell doors had been shut. "What the fuck?" I spoke to no one.

This place was really starting to freak me out, the paranoia feeling was coming back, and something was silently telling me to get the hell out of there. I went back into the office to grab my phone that I had set on the desk. When I looked back at the book, something caught my eye. "Gilbert Lewis, deceased, paid in full." That was a weird combination of words.

I took a moment and actually read through the pages, more and more like the first, though some would say "payment due" or "debt not paid," dozens of names written, dozens deceased, either hanged or shot or poisoned. Next to their names were a few more details regarding their deaths. "Holy shit." No wonder this place is a ghost town.

"Krystal!" a voice called to me; it sounded like Angie. I closed the book and left, not worrying about putting it away. The street was empty, and I couldn't see my friends anywhere. "Krystal." Another call, this one sounded farther, but I couldn't place the direction.

"Angie?" I called back and waited. It became silent again. The wind blew through the street, carrying dirt into my face. I had to shield my eyes from the onslaught.

Through my fingers, I could see the shape of someone on the far side of the town. "Angie!" I called her and headed her way. Instead of meeting me, she ran off to the left. I sighed and followed her, "Angie come on, we need to go." I picked up a jog and followed where she ran.

I jogged through rows of buildings that must have been houses back in the day. I didn't stop to look at them, instead followed Angie in her annoying game of catch-me-if-you-can. Her giggle reached my ears, and I shook my head. "Angie, this is not the place to be playing games." She took another turn, then another, weaving through the buildings giggling at her little game. "Fine, but when I catch you, we're leaving."

I chased after her, picking up speed through the dusty town; I slightly noticed the broken-down houses and an animal skeleton here and there. I groaned as I watched her dodge behind another large building to the right. *Where the hell is she going, and where are Antonio and Dorothy? I thought they were all together.*

I burst around the corner and halted in my tracks. Splayed out were dozens, if not a couple hundred, grave-stones. There had to be a couple of acres full of graves, and who knew how many unmarked ones there may be? Seeing them brought the book back to mind. With all of those names and deaths, another shiver ran down my spine. "Okay, Angie, we should really go." I looked around, but I couldn't see her; where the hell did she go now? "Angie!" I circled my hands around my mouth to call out for her.

I didn't get a response. *Fuck it; I'm just going to wait in the car.* I turned back to the large building to head back to the center. I noticed it was an old church; a bell tower stuck out from the top, but there was no longer a bell that hung there. The windows were broken, and a large hole gaped into the side of the building. Next to the longer side of the church was a platform, a tall bar stuck out and bent at the top like an upside-down L. I gulped down the nervous lump in my throat and continued to walk, not wanting to think of all the men and women that hung there.

This place was a hellhole, and I was ready to go. "Angie, Dorothy, Antonio! Let's go!" I yelled out to them and worked my way back to the car. I could hear voices call back but couldn't make out what they were saying. It took a few minutes, but I was able to weave my way back. Once there, I called again as loudly as I could to get their attention.

"We're coming, we're coming," Dorothy called back, and a few moments later, the three of them appeared behind the school, opposite from where I came from. "This place is pretty boring, but Angie got some cool pictures."

I scoffed, "How could she do that when she was playing chase?" They all looked at me, utterly confused.

"What do you mean?" Angie asked, tilting her head slightly.

"I mean, you had me running after you all over the town not even ten minutes ago. What, did you forget already?" I chuckled and opened the door to get in the driver's seat. They followed but still looked like I was speaking alien. "This place is fucking hell, dude. I found the sheriff's office; you would not believe how crooked he was." I turned on the car and headed back to the main road. "He would blackmail the townspeople; he made them pay him, or he would charge their family members with a crime and have them hanged. And if they still didn't pay, he would bribe the town doctor to poison them." I exaggerated a shiver, remembering the details. "There was a whole ledger with all the details. It was so freaky."

They were quiet for a bit which surprised me, I thought they would be buzzing about the fact. "What do you mean you were chasing me?" Angie asked suddenly, completely ignoring what I had told them.

"Yeah, Angie was with us the whole time," Antonio added, making me about as confused as they looked.

I thought back to the little chase game. "No, you called me while I was in the sheriff's office, I saw you, and you ran off when I tried to meet you. Then you just kept giggling and made me chase you to the cemetery."

Their silence was unnerving. "Krys, I never left Dorothy and Antonio. We never even saw a cemetery," Angie spoke slowly as if she was telling me someone I loved died.

I stayed silent. Then who the hell did I see? Why did they have Angie's laugh and look like her? What the fuck happened? I turned onto the main road, ready to get as far from that place as possible. Dorothy chuckled, "Guess it really is a ghost town."

# THE MINES

I hate working the night shift. I hate being stuck by myself in this creepy-ass place all night. I hate watching over this stupid mine so stupid kids don't try to break in and get themselves hurt. Thankfully, it pays well, and most of the time I just sit on my phone and watch movies or something, but it's the principle of being stuck here.

The mine is an old coal mine that's been running for about 50 years now. The town lives off the mine; we've been thriving from it. Our tourist rates are up, the cost of living in the town is down, and the towns surrounding our little haven have gotten to enjoy the perks of the coal mines as well. There's a sense of pride from working in the mines, and the people in town treat us with a lot of respect. It's an honest living, and I don't mind working with the company; everyone is great, and the owners really look out for the workers, so we never have to worry too much if anyone gets hurt.

I prefer mining, I like having something to do with my hands. I like the honest hard work and the sweat I break into digging and breaking into the earth. I can even handle day shift security, which is ensuring everyone in the mines is safe and no one breaks in to steal the material or tools. Night shift sucks ass. It's now to the point that most of the kids in town don't even come to the mines for their stupid games. They either know better, or their family member works here, and they don't want to get in trouble. So, I'm stuck here watching movies on my phone in the little security trailer, keeping an absent eye on the cameras.

I remember when I was young and did the fear walk. It used to be a town tradition to break into the mining grounds and walk around the tunnels. It was considered a rite of passage if you could go into the mines by yourself and come back with a rock or whatever. It's the main reason we now have security at night; the mines have gotten larger and deeper, and if a kid gets lost or hurt while doing the stupid dare, it would not be good for the company.

I take a drink of my water and take a quick glance at the cameras; there are a few along the fences, the tool shed, and the break area. The mine entrance has a few along the tunnel to the elevator, then there are a bunch throughout the maze of tunnels created over the years. There's little light in the mine cameras, only from the small beam attached to the lens. The full moon illuminates the ones around the fields. Nothing seems out of the ordinary. A few of the field camera movement alerts light up from a small animal running around. I watch a squirrel climb into a tree and fight with another squirrel for a moment. The highlight of my night, I think with a scoff and shake my head.

It's been a long time since I've been on night duty, mostly because I despise it but also because someone preferred it. He's been on night duty for two months now, and the only reason he's out is that he was chasing a kid in the mine, fell on a bunch of tools, and seriously messed himself up. We all got a big talking to about remembering to put away the axes properly the next day, though no one could figure out who left them out in the first place.

When my name was the one called to cover the first night shift, I damn near burst a blood vessel. I had a huge argument with the boss about not wanting to sit by the creepy-ass mine all night. He got this smirk on his face and had the gall to ask, "What, you scared?" No, I'm not scared. The place just creeps me out. They know the history of this place as well as I do.

There's a reason this place was used for a fear walk: it's said to be haunted. About a decade after the mine opened, there was a massive cave-in. Fifteen people died, and about thirty others were seriously injured, my dad being one of them; he had lost his leg. Since then, people have been said to see the ghosts of the men that died walking around and moving the tools to get back to work. I've never personally seen anything, though. To add some heat to the story, an archeologist came by to look at the caves for a project or something about ten years ago. He was accompanied by some of the crew to look at the deeper parts of the mine, trying to find fossils or study the earth, I guess.

Well, they had broken down another area of the mine, and it led to a cave with another entrance to the other side of the mountain. There were Native American paintings on the cave walls, and according to the archeologist, they were sacred symbols meaning the cave was a sacred place. So basically, he was saying we were digging up sacred Native American land. The town didn't like the idea that we had been doing that; some even said we should shut down the mine before things got worse. Yeah, like they'd ever let that happen.

It was a bunch of hocus pocus; they closed the hole they blew into the cave and made sure no one mined that way. The only bad thing that has really happened was the cave-in. I mean, there have been a few things here and there; people get hurt from the axes or a rock falling, you know, typical mining injuries, nothing paranormal. Do I still get creeped out? Yeah, but so would anyone alone in the middle of a mountain and a tunnel of mines that seem to make their own noises due to the wind.

I agreed to night duty tonight if I didn't have to do it again, and I got my wish. I'm almost out of here, too; it's two AM, the grounds are quiet, and honestly, I can probably take a nap. The light of the motion detector alert catches my eye, however. It's one from inside the mine. I quirk my eyebrow and move to focus the computer screen on the camera. It's one from below, meaning whatever little creature it is, had climbed down the elevator shaft. It's rare, but it happens sometimes. Nothing appears out of the ordinary on the camera, so I back out of it so the computer shows the grid of camera views.

My heart nearly jumps out of my chest as I do; one of the other cameras shows the tail end of a person walking passed and out of camera view. "What the fuck?" I say out loud and try to find the person. What's most confusing is that none of the other cameras alerted me to anyone moving around, or maybe they did and I just didn't see. Fuck, I'm in so much trouble. I scroll through the cameras but can't find another figure; they have to have shown up on another one by now, but I can't find them.

I must be seeing things, I'm so damn tired, and the eeriness has gotten me paranoid. I sigh and rub the tired out of my eyes. I look up and scroll to the next camera. "The hell?" The figure's back. This time, it's standing near the base of the elevator, just standing there. It doesn't move as I watch, doesn't get on the elevator to come back up, doesn't move further into the mine, just stands where I found it, staring at the camera. That's all it does; it stares at the camera as if it can see me watching it. I can't make out the features very well, but I can see the lines of its face and a weird glow in its eyes looking back at me.

I take a shaky breath, not quite sure why I feel like it's watching me back. We sit there, neither of us moving. I wait for it to come up the elevator and finish whatever dare they had been given, but the only movement I can catch is a slight tilt of its head, like a dog hearing a new noise. The motion causes my heart to beat so hard that I think it's going to burst. Why is this scaring me so much? It's probably just a kid. A kid I need to get out of the mines. He's probably staring at the cameras trying to get my attention.

I sigh and rub my eyes again; it's too late for this.

When I look back at the camera, the figure is completely gone. I huff and move back to scroll through the cameras trying to find the idiot kid who decided walking through dangerous mines would be a good idea. I scroll and scroll but, again, I can't find him. It's like he's purposefully avoiding the cameras. I groan out my frustration and decide I should go down and get him.

I move the cameras back to a grid, hoping the full view will help me find him. I scream at the face in the corner camera. It's so close to the lens I can finally see its features. My stomach sinks to my shoes, looking at the disfigured thing looking back at me. It doesn't have eyelids, its bloody eyes nearly popping out of their sockets as it stares through the camera into my soul. The tip of its nose is gone, and the bottom lip looks like it had been ripped off.

I shoot up from my chair, causing it to fall back. Is that the person stuck in the mines? Did he get hurt? The fuck happened to his face? I blink finally, and the face is gone. The cameras are once again empty, and I'm left breathing heavily as my eyes rake over the computer screens, trying to find him again.

"Fuck." I whisper, grabbing my gear and heading out to the mine entrance. I turn on my heavy-duty flashlight, illuminating the entire opening. "Hello?" I call into the mine, not seeing anything. The kid's at the bottom; I need to go down. I take a deep breath and walk further in, keeping my light steady so it can light up everything in front of me. The elevator comes into view, the cart still at the top.

A shudder runs through me, and I can't keep my breath from shaking as I open the crate and get in, pressing the button to go down. The machine whirs to life and clanks loudly before leading me down into the pit. I can't hear anything over the rattling of the elevator as I go down. Once I'm down and can see into the tunnel, I call out again, "Hello, is anyone down here?" With the elevator quiet, I can hear again, though it's silent through the tunnel aside from the wind whistling against the cave walls. I strain to listen, trying to hear whatever voice might be there.

I walk further into the tunnel, my light shining until the bend in the earth cuts off my view. My breath shakes with each step; where can the kid be? "Is anyone down here? Are you hurt?" I call, my voice echoing. Still, I hear nothing. I sigh and keep walking until one tunnel turns into three, shit which way now. "Is anyone down there?" I call into the tunnels. I wait, listening for an answer.

"Help." It's faint, but I can hear the call back. "Help." I focus on the faint voice and follow it down the right tunnel, the one that goes to the deepest part of the mine. Of course, the little idiot would go down there. I steel my nerve and continue. It starts becoming colder, and the air is damp, causing me to shiver as I wave my light around, looking for an injured kid.

The tunnel continues to be empty as I go. "Call out again; I can't find you!" I yell for the kid. That nightmarish face is still in the forefront of my mind, and I'm trying to figure out how I'll react if I see the poor kid's face up close. How could something like that even happen down here? I didn't notice any rock fall, and all our equipment is packed away. It's probably something I'd prefer to stay a mystery.

"Down here, I'm down here." Again, the voice sounds dim and far away, but I can hear it bounce against the cave walls. He must be at the end of the tunnel or something.

"Can you walk? Can you walk to me?" I don't want to go much further, to be honest. I keep getting this feeling down my spine that's telling me to turn away.

"Down here, help." I'll take that as a no. I sigh and ignore the feeling, going after the voice. How much further can they possibly be? I'm nearing the end of the tunnel, based on the markers on the walls. If he isn't right here, then... I don't know what to think. I round another corner and find a bunch of wooden beams blocking the path, a large sign stating "DO NOT PASS" on it. The kid is nowhere to be seen.

"The fuck?" I look around the thinning tunnel as if I missed him. I know I heard the voice coming from down here. I groan and look back at the boards. I notice, then, an opening in the bottom corner large enough for someone to get through. "You gotta be kidding me," I grumble and crouch down to the opening. I flash my light into the hole but can't see much from my angle. "Are you in there?" I call in.

A moan comes from the other side; it sounds pained like he's in so much pain that he can't speak anymore. "Shit," I mumble. I push my light through the hole and get down to crawl through. I can just barely get through, squeezing in and pulling the rest of my body past the barrier. I sigh once I'm through and grab my light again. This is an area I've never seen before. It's a large cave, rounded almost fifty feet in diameter. "Holy shit," comes out in a whisper as my light sweeps the walls. With it, I can see ancient paintings, mostly of animals: a snake, some kind of bird, a fish, and some others I can't make out because of their age.

It takes me a moment to realize where I am; the moment I do, I suck in a breath and nearly book it to the beams. This is the cave the archeologist had found, the sacred one. I quickly look around, trying to find the damn kid and get the hell out, but I'm alone. I run my fingers through my hair, trying to get my head straight. I know I heard someone in here; there was a voice. I shake my head and run to the entrance. Screw this, fuck all of this; I am done!

I throw my light through the opening and follow, pushing my body along the ground and grunting as my mid-waist gets caught slightly. I pull through just for something to grab my legs and pull me back to the other side. My scream travels through the cave, and I kick at whatever the hell is grabbing me. My feet never connect with anything, but I am let go and rush to get back to the other side.

As soon as I get to my feet, I grab my light and run through the cave. "NOO!" A scream follows behind me, pushing my legs faster through the dirt. I round a corner and a bend and another, following the main tunnel. Over the sound of my own panting and the thumping of my feet hitting the soil, another pair of footsteps follow. My adrenaline goes into overdrive, pushing me faster through the tunnel and back to safety.

I get back to the fork in the tunnels. Which way, which way? I can't think properly. I'm so scared, the feet behind me getting closer, and I try to remember which way to go. Shit! I went right to get down here, so I must go left. I make the quick decision to take the far-left tunnel and make the mistake of looking behind me before I do.

I see a mangled figure racing after me; I catch it for only a moment before I rush around the corner. Its limbs, dressed in old mining clothes, went in the wrong direction as it ran, that face, the nightmarish face, staring into me and yelling something incoherent from its messed-up mouth. "Fuck!" I scream. I can't get out fast enough. I can barely see where I'm going from the flailing of the flashlight.

The elevator comes into view, and I feel relief wash over me. I run into the cart and slam the door shut, smashing the up button until the machine whirs back to life. Something between a laugh and a sob bursts from me as the cart starts moving up. A glimpse of the nightmare thing is the last thing I see before the earth surrounds the cart. I crouch, catching my breath for a moment, letting the relief wash over me, the adrenaline starts to wear off, and my body shakes with every breath.

The elevator clanks as it hooks into place at the top of the mine; I quickly leave the cart and run the best I can out of the mine. I'm not safe until I'm out. The breath I take as I leave the mouth is full of a freshness I've never felt before. My feet continue to carry me away from the mine, away from the nightmare thing, until I'm safe in the security trailer. I slouch in the chair, and exhaustion takes hold of me. I feel like I'm going to pass out as the adrenaline leaves my body. I don't even want to look at the cameras, afraid I'm going to see that thing again. I turn off the computer screens without looking and let myself sag in my chair. God, I really hate working the night shift.

# APPALACIA

We spent the weekend at this cabin in the woods. I know that's how all horror stories start, but this was, for real, the creepiest thing to ever happen to me. It was me, my girlfriend Syd, and our friends Brian and Jamie. We decided to have a couple's weekend in the mountains. A getaway to strengthen our relationships, or whatever the girls were thinking. It's not like there was anything wrong with our relationship. They just wanted an excuse to go to an isolated cabin in the deep mountains of West Virginia.

It was a beautiful weekend, though, a nice spring day. The temperature was perfect, which was great considering we had to hike up to the cabin for almost two hours. If I had known there'd be that much hiking, I probably wouldn't have agreed to come. Though, if I'd known more about what this weekend would hold, I would've laughed in their faces.

We met our guide Friday morning at the ranger station. He was a nice guy named Steven. He gave us some tips on handling the great outdoors: make sure you drown your fire so it doesn't spread; if a bear shows up, keep calm and don't spook it; if something happens with the electricity, call this number.

Though, he wasn't the only one trying to give us advice. An older gentleman was sitting in the ranger's station, he had long grey hair pulled back in a braid, and he looked Native with his tan skin and high bone structure. "Be very careful in the mountains. Never go out into the woods after dark, no matter what you hear or see. If you hear something; no, you didn't. If someone calls, don't respond. And never walk around alone."

I felt like laughing but I didn't want to appear disrespectful. "Thanks for the advice." Brian laughed and headed out. Like myself, he didn't take that stuff seriously; it's all superstition, there isn't anything actually in the woods. There're no such things as monsters.

The last thing I heard before leaving the station was the old man saying, "I'll pray for your souls." It sent a weird chill down my spine. The walk took forever, it didn't help that we were carrying our heavy bags all the way. Steven pointed out some of the things in nature as we went up: the different plants, and what poison ivy looks like, and he pointed out a family of foxes further into the forest. He always ensured we never fell too far behind "Don't need anyone getting lost around here."

The cabin wasn't too bad. It was a classic wooden cabin with a comfortable living area open to a kitchen. The dining room table sat in between the two spaces. A short hallway led to two bedrooms and a bathroom. It was pretty cozy inside, and plenty of space between the trees allowed for a picnic table, grill, and fire pit out front. Overall, not bad. However, there wasn't any cable or cell service. My phone couldn't pick up any bars, and the box of a TV only had a VHS slot.

"If you need anything else, call us with the landline; the emergency numbers are on the fridge." He started heading out but stopped. "And what Mr. Redman said at the station, please listen to him. There's some freaky stuff that happens in these woods at night." He gave a tight smile and headed out.

Brian laughed when he was gone. "Man, is everyone around here superstitious? Oooh, scary ghosts." He moaned like he was impersonating a ghost before bending over with laughter.

Jamie hit him on the shoulder. "Will you stop? They both seem pretty serious. I've heard of a lot of freaky shit that happens in the Appalachians." She shuddered as she sat on the old floral couch.

I sat on one of the other chairs; it was surprisingly comfortable. "I just can't believe all of that, you know. There're no such things as ghosts and monsters." Syd sat on my lap, and I wrapped my arms around her waist. "They probably just say that stuff to scare people away from exploring after dark and getting lost."

The first day went great. Brian was the champ who brought the coolers with all the food and booze. We grilled some burgers and enjoyed the fire. I didn't miss the internet, surprisingly. I couldn't remember the last time I had enjoyed myself like this, just being outside and hanging out with my friends. It was refreshing.

The night came almost too quickly. We stayed by the

fire for a while, drinking beers and looking up at the clear, starry sky. It was always so bright back home that we never got to see them. "Should we tell ghost stories," Brian asked, a little tipsy.

"Go for it," Syd said, sipping her beer.

Brian stood up like he was about to present to the class and cleared his throat. "It was a dark night in the woods." He started.

"Boo!" the girls shouted. "That's how every ghost story starts." Jamie finished.

"Let me finish." He whined before correcting himself. "It was a dark night in the woods. Like us, a group of friends were camping deep in the forest. A bunch of teenagers just having a good time. But they didn't know that it was the anniversary of Shannie Blake's death.

"Shannie?" Syd snorted with a laugh.

"Hush. Shannie Blake was a mother of two boys. One day she came home and found her husband, the father of her kids, in bed with her best friend. She was so enraged that she became insane. She took her two boys into that very forest and drowned them in the lake, not too far from where those kids were camping. It wasn't until they were dead that she realized what she had done. She was so distraught and ashamed that she drowned herself in the same lake.

"The police found them a week later, their bodies already dissolving from the water." Jamie gagged at the mental image. "But even though they took the bodies, their spirits stayed in the woods – the boys running away from their mother for fear of getting hurt again.

"It's said that on the anniversary of their deaths, Shannie would go looking for her boys, and anyone who got in her way would be punished and drowned, too. This was the legend those kids had heard, but they thought they were safe because they believed the anniversary was months away."

"Dumb kids," Syd interjected. I chuckled and kept listening.

"It was about midnight, and one of the friends got up from their little circle around the fire to go to the bathroom. He walked away from the group far enough that it was too dark to see what was in front of him. Before he could even unzip his pants, he heard a voice. It was quiet; it sounded like crying. The kid thought it was one of his friends messing with him, so he ignored it. This is until it was right next to his ear: 'Help me,' it said. He whipped around, but there was no one there.

"He thought he was going crazy for a second; maybe it was the wind. Then he heard it again, louder, 'Help me;' It was further away, but it was calling to him. He called, 'Hello?' and saw someone moving in the trees. Like the stupid kid he is, he follows the movement away from his friends. He continued to hear the voices call, 'Help me, help me;' he kept following it, sure it was real now.

"He ended up at a lake, so big he couldn't see the other side in the moonlight. There was no one around; It was too quiet, no voices, no wind, hell, even the sounds of the animals stopped. He looked around for the voice's owner, even calling out again, 'Hello, anyone there?' No answer.

"He finally decided he was crazy and probably too tired, so he turned around to head back to his friends. But as he turned, something grabbed his ankle, keeping him there. He looked down, and around his ankle was a ghostly wet hand. His chest became heavy as he pulled his leg, trying to break free, but the hand had a vise grip. He turned around, panting in fear to see who was holding him.

"Still halfway in the water was a woman's body. Her long black hair covered her face, a white dress was torn on her body, and the parts of her skin showing were decaying and falling off. Her left arm reached out and held onto his ankle tightly. He screamed and tried to run, but her grip was too tight he just fell. He felt her pulling and watched her sink back into the lake, dragging him with her. He screamed for help and clawed at the ground, trying to escape. 'Help me, help me,' he screamed like the voices he heard.

"The cold water slowly started surrounding him. He tried and tried, but he couldn't get away. Soon the water engulfed his head, and as he looked at the surface as he was being pulled to the bottom, he saw the silhouette of two young children watching him drown.

"It was getting late, and his friends knew they should look for him, but they were too scared to go out into the woods. 'Let's look for him tomorrow; I'm sure he's fine,' one of the friends said, and they all agreed; the little cowards. Come the morning, they looked around for him but couldn't find a trace of him. They looked and looked through the forest and around the lake. But they couldn't find anything." He paused for a moment. "They found him in the lake a week later. His body was decomposing, but there was still a bruise around his ankle in the shape of a hand."

He finished then, and the group was silent for a moment. "Wow, that was actually kind of creepy," Jamie said, and we all laughed. "I'm getting tired. I'm gonna head to bed." She got up and walked into the cabin.

"I'm with you," Syd stated and followed her in.

"We'll be in in a second." I let her know. I took the final swig of my beer and stood. "Let's drown the fire and head to bed." It was already going down, so luckily, it didn't take much to kill it completely.

We headed into the cabin and got ready for bed. Syd was already asleep by the time I got in. I changed and got into the bed next to her before falling asleep.

I wasn't sure if I was dreaming or not that night. I felt like I was dreaming, my body was heavy, and my mind was fuzzy, but I could see the cabin. I was looking at everything: the ceiling, the brown walls. I could feel the sheets on my body and the weight of Syd lying next to me. *Maybe I am awake, and I just can't move. Is this what sleep paralysis is?* I didn't like it. I tried what I could to move, but I couldn't get my body to budge. After a few minutes, I gave up and tried to go back to sleep.

It was hard, though, with all the noises. It wasn't your normal nightly sounds like bats and wind. It sounded like it should be the wind, but there was something with it, like a high-pitched whine, but the tone moved. It turned from a whine to a moan to a scream and back again. I thought I could hear it saying something. "It's here; help me, come to me." At some moments, I could hear it call my name, "Daniel." I just kept my eyes closed; it was just a dream.

The noises went on all night, the wind whining and calling out, "Daniel, Daniel!" With each call, it sounded like it was getting closer until it was right outside the window. I still refused to open my eyes, until the banging came. The hit came to the window, and I could hear the crack of the glass. My eyes bolted open, and I looked around the room, still unable to move my body. I tried to look at the window; maybe a bird or a bat hit it. I could just barely see it out of the corner of my eye. The was something there. I could only make out a black shape at the bottom of the window, nothing more. Maybe it was a little bat that crashed into the window, poor thing.

But then there was more noise, another hit on the window but nothing to hit it. Then the sound traveled right, towards the back where our heads were. Slowly, *bang, bang, bang.* Each hit moved closer to our heads. The only other noise I could hear was the rush of my heartbeat filling my ears. Syd lay still next to me; how the banging wasn't waking her, I couldn't understand. I still couldn't force my body to move; I was just stuck there, listening to each hit get closer to my head. Then it came, the loudest and eeriest. The bang came with a woman's scream, "LET ME IN."

I was finally able to move. I jolted up and turned around to face the window behind our heads. It was clear, the moon slightly illuminating the dark woods behind the house, no figure, no animals. No one screaming at me. My body shook as I looked at all the windows to ensure nothing was there; I couldn't tell if it was from fear or the cold sweat that ran over my body. I got up and went to the kitchen to grab some water.

I sighed and sat on the couch. That was a super freaky dream; if that's what sleep paralysis was, I never wanted to experience it again. It was the first time it ever happened and in a freaky cabin of all places. Such a freaky night, first those weird warnings from the old man and then the creepy ghost story from Brian, and now this dream. What a night. I sat back on the couch and chugged down the water.

To make matters worse, I forgot about the super ghoulish portraits they had spread around the living room. It was like someone dug up corpses and thought 'Hey, these would be pretty interesting to paint.' Who would hang these in this kind of place? I looked at each of them. One was a woman with her flesh peeling from her body, pieces of bone and muscle sticking out, and her eyes melting out of their sockets. Somehow it felt like she was still staring down into my soul.

The next looked more demonic than human. I couldn't tell if it was a man or woman; the jawbone hung down to the chest, its tongue hanging loose. There was no skin, just strips of thin muscle over withering bone. Its eyes were still there, staring down and watching from its skinless face.

The third was charred like it had been burned. The

black flesh was chipping off, and red lines were cracking through it as if a fire was still blazing underneath. Its face was nothing but empty holes. Looking at it made me feel hot, a new layer of sweat forming over my skin as if I was there in the fire, too.

The last, the one right in front of me, felt the worst. It was another woman; her black hair was wet and sticking to her frame. The skin was blue and bubbling off, parts of her bloated, and the flesh goopy, like it had become pudding. Her eyes remained, and they looked straight ahead into mine.

How could anyone paint things like this? How could the people that own this place put them in here, where people are, where children could be? They were terrifying, but I couldn't stop looking at them. I felt them staring back, their gaze seeping into my soul. I started to feel weird and anxious, like nausea boiling in my chest. I wanted to move back into my room, but I felt stuck again, but this time I knew I wasn't dreaming. I took a deep breath and forced myself to stand up and walk away from the living room.

"Daniel." A voice whispered, drawing me back into the living room. I looked around and saw there wasn't anyone there. I must really need to go back to bed. I shook my head and turned around, only for a knock to come to the door. That feeling of dread hit me again, the one from earlier in bed. I stood frozen, listening to another knock on the door. "Daniel." Someone called from behind it. My breathing shook as I turned to the door.

*This isn't real, right? I'm dreaming again. It's like three in the morning; there is no way someone is knocking on the door all the way up here.* I took a step towards the door, then another, my heart pounding like a gong as I got closer. The voice on the other end came more, banging on the door with each call. I stood right in front of the door, my hand shaking as it reached for the knob. It was like I was in a trance; I couldn't break out of it. The voice was making me come to it and let it in.

"*If something calls your name, don't follow it.*" The old man's voice found its way into my head, and it felt like a band snapped my brain. I fell onto the floor and crawled backward. The banging became louder and more frequent, the voice calling, "Daniel, Daniel, let me in." It grew louder and louder until it felt like it was banging inside my skull.

My heartbeat was too fast; I felt like it would burst. My breath became rough and shallow, and I couldn't stand it anymore. I was trapped, helpless, terrified. "Go away!" I screamed at the faceless thing that was threatening my sanity.

Suddenly everything stopped. The banging, the voices, the dread, it all went away. "Daniel?" The voice was so close that I yelled and crawled backward from it. The lights burst on, and I could finally see clearly. Syd stood in the doorway of our bedroom, rubbing her eyes. "Baby, what are you doing? Are you okay?"

I could only imagine how I looked, sweating like a marathon runner, shaking, and probably crazed in the eyes from the terror. I looked back at the door and then at her. "Um, yeah, yeah."

She walked over and kneeled next to me. "What happened, baby?" She brushed my sweaty hair out of my face.

"Yeah, um, yeah, just a dream, I think." I stood up with a bit of help from Syd.

"A dream? Did you sleepwalk or something? You've never done that before." She held my arm and looked up at me with concern. "You wanna talk about it?"

I shook my head. "Not right now. Maybe in the morning." She nodded, and we went back into the bedroom. "Do you think we can keep the light on? The dream freaked me out." She smiled and gave me a quick kiss before agreeing. I was surprised I could fall back asleep so quickly and stayed asleep until sunrise.

I stood staring into the living area. I felt the dread come back but for a whole different reason. I knew I was awake last night in here. I knew I was; even with all the weird voices and banging, I was awake. I hadn't imagined anything, right? But when I looked into the living room and looked at the area those portraits were – those terrifying portraits of what I could only believe were spawns of hell – only stood clear windows that looked out into the forest.

Was it all a dream, everything? From the wind to the banging on the door. I felt the rush of my heart again, but this time I felt like I was going crazy. I couldn't believe what was happening; I couldn't understand anything. I felt like I was awake last night, but if I was awake, then what I saw was real. I was spiraling. I felt ... like I was in danger somehow. Those things, whatever they were, they were after me, calling to me, trying to get in. They called my name, trying to get me to come out.

It was real; it was all real. Is everything real? Ghosts, monsters, they're real? My head spun as I felt my life do a complete one-eighty as I learned that everything I thought I knew was wrong. "We need to leave." I blurted out suddenly.

The room went quiet as they paused making breakfast. "What do you mean?" Syd asked from the table.

"We need to go; we can't stay here another night." I knew how I sounded, but I couldn't take the idea of being here again with those things.

"Dude, did my story freak you out last night?" Brian laughed and pulled the eggs off the pan.

"Listen, this is gonna sound nuts, but something happened last night." They looked at me with confusion. "I thought I was asleep, but I know I wasn't. There were things; they were right outside those windows, looking right at me. They called to me and were banging on the door and the walls. It was terrifying, man."

They were quiet for a second before Brian started laughing. "Sounds like you had too much to drink last night."

"Dude, no! Do you really think I would make something like this up? Me?" They grew quiet again at that. "Listen, I know how it sounds; trust me, I'm having a hard time believing it myself, but I know what I saw." I looked back towards the windows; I could almost make out the imprint of those torturing faces.

"I believe you," Jamie spoke up. "I was hearing a lot of weird stuff last night. I thought it was a dream, but I didn't feel like I was dreaming. I could hear voices calling to me; it sounded like my mom." She wrung her hands around her coffee cup. "If you don't think we're safe, if you think something is out there, then maybe you're right and we should leave."

I sighed with a bit of relief. "Fine, fine, we'll go. Let's finish breakfast, and then we'll go." Brian agreed.

We got out of there quickly enough. Luckily nothing was unpacked, and we just needed to put the food away. The walk back down wasn't too bad, the weather was still nice, and it went a lot faster since it was downhill.

When we arrived back at the ranger's station, we were greeted by the two gentlemen that were there yesterday. Steven looked confused as we walked in. "You guys are back early. I thought you were staying the whole weekend?"

Syd shrugged, "Change of plans. Something's come up." She smiled and handed him back the key to the cabin.

I felt eyes on me again, and I looked over at the old man. "You saw something, didn't you?" He looked straight at me as he spoke. "Something came to you, called out to you, didn't it?"

My throat went dry, but I nodded. "They looked like death and kept calling me to let them in." Everyone went quiet and listened.

The old man nodded and sat back more in his chair. "Be glad you didn't." That was all he said.

The dread came back slightly from the statement. But driving away from the mountain, I felt more at ease. I was happy to be going back to the city, away from whatever those things were. There are still times I have nightmares where I see those faces staring down at me, but at least now I know they're dreams. And I will never go back into the woods.

# OLD WOOD

Finally, I got my own bachelor pad! Yeah, I know that's stupid to say, but I finally have a place I can call my own – no parents, no roommates, just me. It's a nice little place on the water, with two beds, one bath; a quaint little two-floor brick house. I got it for a steal, too, because it needs a ton of work that I am totally ready to do. Thankfully, it's all cosmetic; if the foundation were fucked I would be, too.

I moved in about two weeks ago, and I had already started on the renovations. I'm thankful that my grandparents set aside a "life account" or whatever it's called for when I got my own place. There was enough for the house and the renovations I would need. I started with the kitchen; it was seriously built in the 50s. Everything was getting worn down, and the wood had a smell to it that I couldn't place. I was excited to gut the thing and put my flare on it. I got cool gray cabinets and new dark hardwood floors; it would look so good when I finished.

I have to say, though, this house makes a lot of fucking noise. It's kept me awake most nights as the pipes and old wood settled in the middle of the night. There were so many creaks and groans coming from all over, but primarily the attic. I have yet to go up there; I'm saving it for last because I know if there's room and it's not finished, I would turn it into something and waste all my money on it. By the way it creaks, I feel like it might be one of those attics where there isn't any space and a lot of asbestos; maybe I should check it out. Nah, they wouldn't sell the house if it was filled with asbestos.

I've gotten to become good friends with a couple of my neighbors. It's a friendly community where all the neighbors know each other, and they have block parties every summer, so I've been able to make the connections I need. There's Bonnie and Joe, the elderly couple at the end of the block. When I first moved in, she brought me a welcome pie and let me know that if I ever needed any-thing, to just ask. The Miltons, who live kitty-corner to me, have been really helpful with some of the heavy lifting. Teddy, the husband, saw me struggling with get-ting my cabinets in the house and gave me a hand. Lily has been bringing me dinner plates every now and then, too.

I'm really loving the neighborhood and the house, even with the creaks and the crap ton of work, it's be-coming a passion project to get it just the way I like. I've taken a month off work to get done what I needed; I'm glad I saved up all that PTO. I can get the bigger things done, like the kitchen, and redoing all the floors and walls.

It was the middle of the third week, and it was a hot August day, so I was taking a rest from the extra heavy work, opting to paint the walls. I had picked this nice light blue-gray color that went well with the furniture. I spent the morning getting all the paint and supplies and dedicated the day to painting as many rooms as possible. I finished up the living room and the hallways on the first floor before I was ready for lunch.

Almost as if on cue, the door knocked. I opened it and smiled at my new friends. Teddy, Lily, and their ten-year-old daughter Hannah were at the door. Hannah had a basket filled with tubs and bags of food. "We saw you with a bunch of stuff this morning, and we wanted to make you some lunch," Lily explained, and Hannah held out the basket with a bright smile.

It was so heartwarming to have such kind neighbors. "I really appreciate it, thank you. Would you like to come in?" I stepped to the side, and they filed in. "Just be careful of the walls; they're still drying." I shut the door behind them, and they took a seat on the couch pushed into the center of the room. Hannah held out the basket to me again, and I took it, grinning. "Thanks, sweet pea." I peered into the basket a little more. They made a lot of food. "Would you like to stay for lunch? I'm definitely not gonna eat all of this by myself."

We shared a chuckle, and they agreed. I grabbed some paper plates from the kitchen and a few glasses to pour some lemonade. It was a delicious lunch; we talked a bit, getting to know each other more. "You are quite a lot nicer than our last neighbor; he was a bit of a grump," Lily said, sipping her lemonade.

"The guy who lived here before?" I asked, and they nodded. "Was he like really mean?"

Lily shook her head. "He wasn't mean per se, but he wasn't very social and didn't like people in the house. He was here long before we moved into the neighborhood. In fact, I think this was the first house built; all the other houses around here were built in the 70s, I think."

"Yeah, the realtor said the house was built in 1954." I took a bite of the pasta salad they made; it was so good. I might have to have them teach me the recipes for all this.

"He wasn't a horrible man, but anytime anyone tried to greet him or offer to help him out with something, he kind of got this sour look on his face and would say something along the lines of 'I don't need your help, I don't need anyone, leave me alone.' Eventually, we just let him be and let anyone new to the neighborhood know not to bother him." Teddy added with a shrug.

I nodded, listening; it explained why the house was so out of date. If it were lived in by an elderly man who might not have been able to care for it, I wouldn't be surprised if it turned into crap. I'm thankful it's not any worse. "What happened? How come he moved out?"

They took a drink from their cups. "He passed away sometime a few months ago," Lily stated, and it became silent for a moment. "He didn't have any family, not that we know of. The bank bought the house up, and everything got sold in an estate sale about a month before you moved in."

I nodded and took a drink of my own lemonade. I figured that with this place's age, at least one person may have died in it or while living here. It's just a little surreal to hear it. "Did he die in the house, do you know?" My realtor didn't tell me, and I'm pretty sure they're required to let you know if someone died in the house.

They both shook their heads. "No, I found him having a heart attack outside and called an ambulance. He died at the hospital," Teddy informed me. I felt my shoulders relax, feeling a little better that he didn't die in the house.

The rest of the lunch had lighter topics. Hannah told me all about the school play she participated in in the spring, she was Gretel in Hansel and Gretel, and she was excited to do another one. She wants to be an actress when she grows up because she loves playing pretend. It was a comforting conversation; I have a younger sister who was born ten years after me, so I'm used to the excited mind of a little girl.

After everyone had gotten their fill and the conversations died down, they announced they would be leaving. "Oh, do you happen to have a power drill I could borrow? My batteries have gone kaput, and I have a small project I need to get done. I'm gonna order a new battery, but I wanted to ask if it was okay." Teddy asked before he walked out of the door.

"Of course, let me go grab it." I went into the kitchen and grabbed the pack that held my power drill and its accessories. "Here you go." I handed it to him, and he smiled.

"I really appreciate it; thank you so much. I'll get it back to you tomorrow."

I waved it off. "You guys have been incredible to me since I moved in; borrowing a tool is no big deal, and use it as long as you need. I'll work on other stuff until you're done." I returned the smile, and after a few more thank yous Teddy left and I returned to my silent home. Now it was too quiet without the company. I took out my phone and connected it to the speaker sitting next to the TV. I picked out a playlist and let it play as I cleaned up the table and returned to work painting.

I spent the next few hours painting up the stairwell and the second-floor hallway. I brought the speaker up so I could hear the music better. *Which room should I do next? I asked myself. It's probably wise to do my room next so it's dry by the time I'm ready for bed.* I ran downstairs to switch out the roller and brushes to clean ones and let the dirty ones soak in hot water.

On my way back up, I notice something weird in the paint in the hallway between the kitchen and living room. It looked like a handprint and some smear. Where the hell did that come from? I tried to think back, Hannah did walk to the kitchen at one point, but she didn't seem like the type not to say anything; I also didn't notice any paint on her hands. I was stumped trying to figure out how the handprint got there, but I eventually just shook my head and grabbed a bit of the paint to fix it. Once fixed, I took the clean tools up to my room to begin there.

I loved the color I painted my room; it's a pale green, not like a lemon green but more of a foam green. It looked nice once I was done. I looked at the clock and saw it was about six in the evening. I think now is a good time to stop for the night, get something to eat, and relax. I ordered a pizza and changed into not-gross clothes before settling on the couch. I turned on the TV and decided to take some time and scroll through my phone.

I got a text from my mom not too long after, mostly asking how I was, how's the house, do I need anything, the works. I texted her back that everything was great. She asked then if I still had some pictures from Molly's dance recital and if I could send them to her. I chuckled and went to my photos to see if I could find them.

I scrolled through my albums, found them, and sent them to her. Before I closed it out, a picture caught my eye. I scrunched my eyebrows as I opened it and couldn't tell if I should be shocked, confused, or scared. The photo was of me laying in bed fast asleep. From the lack of natural light from the window, it was some time at night. It wouldn't have creeped me out so much if it was from my previous living situations, but it was from this house. It was in my room upstairs. I couldn't think of any rational explanation. Did someone break into my house just to take a picture of me with my own phone? That seems highly unlikely, so why the fuck was this picture here!

I decided I didn't want to think about it and deleted the photo. *There, like it never happened.* I sighed and looked back up at the TV; some food show was playing. A loud bang at the door made me jump and wonder for a second who could be there, and then I remembered I ordered pizza. I opened the door, and the bored-looking teenager handed me my pizza. I gave him the payment with his tip, and no words were spoken before he left.

The rest of the night went by boring and uneventful. I went to bed at around ten after watching a few movies. The walls were mostly dry, but I still felt uncomfortable pushing the furniture back. So, I just slept with the bed in the middle of the room. I must have been exhausted because even with all of the creaks and groans, I fell asleep faster than I have since moving here.

It was the weekend, a time for relaxation. It was the weekend before school started again, so the neighborhood kids were running around and doing whatever they could before they had to go back. I was sitting on the front porch stairs and having a quick beer. The sun wasn't as hot, so it was nice enough to sit outside. I had finished the painting and redid all the floors on the first floor the last few days, so I was taking a longer break before getting back to it. I was also waiting for my drill so I could finish the kitchen, but there was no rush on it.

I was also taking a break because I was so damn tired. I had the hardest time falling asleep last night. I kept having weird dreams, and those damn noises wouldn't stop. In my exhausted state, they turned into a pattern, *squeak, groan, squeak, groan,* like a chair rocking back and forth all night long. Though when I tried to focus on the noise, it lost the pattern.

I rubbed my tired eyes and looked out at the neighborhood. Then I got lost in looking at the lawn; I desperately needed to mow it. The grass had gotten a bit overgrown, and the wooden fence was dirty as could be and had vines growing up the beams. That's the next project, getting this lawn under control. "Afternoon, neighbor!" I looked up to see Teddy walking through the open gate. I smiled and stood to welcome him. "Finally, bringing back your drill. Sorry, it took so long; stuff kind of got in the way." He looked embarrassed.

I shook my head. "No worries, man. Hey, do you wanna come in for a beer or something?" I felt like having some company since I've been pretty alone the last few days.

"Thanks, but I don't want to bother your guest or anything." I blanched at his statement. What the hell was he talking about?

"Guest?" I asked incredulously.

He pointed up at the top window. "Your guest." I followed his hand and felt my stomach sink when I saw a figure in the window. I couldn't see any features, but the shape was very distinct.

My blood felt frozen as I stared. "I don't have a guest." I ran into the house, planning to catch the person who broke in. I could hear Teddy following me as I raced up the stairs. The window belonged to my room. I burst in expecting to see a man standing there, but there was nothing. I looked all over: in the closet, and the bath-room, Teddy helped me look around the rest of the house, but there was no way whoever was in there would have been able to get out without us seeing them. I sat on my bed, utterly confounded. I looked up at Teddy, who looked just as confused. "You saw it, too, right?"

"I'm the one who pointed it out; I would have sworn

on my life that someone was in that window." He ran his fingers through his blonde hair and looked around as though he was expecting the figure to appear again. "Where would he have gone?"

I shrugged and repeated his motion. "I have no clue; there's no way he would have made it down the stairs without us seeing or hearing him." I sighed and shook my head. "This house has been weird, man." This all made me think of the photo on my phone. "I was looking through my phone the other day, and there was a picture of me sleeping. It was in this house; I was freaked out."

He looked at me like I had two heads. "Someone took a picture of you sleeping? With your own phone?" I nodded and pulled it out. It should still be in my deleted files. I opened my photos app and sucked in a breath. "What the fuck?" There were two more pictures in the recents album. One was of me sleeping with the bed in the middle of the room; the other was during the day, and my back was turned as I was placing down the floorboards.

Teddy came over to look at my phone. "That's fucking creepy. And you didn't notice anyone?"

I shook my head. "There is no way anyone could've come in without me knowing, especially if I was awake. This house creaks like nobody's business." I looked at the pictures again, trying to get some sort of understanding.

Teddy chuckled a bit, and I looked up at him, shocked; why was he laughing? "Maybe the place is haunted." He smirked as he said it, and I knew he was joking, but that's not fun to think about.

"Don't joke about that, man; that freaks me out." I hate the idea of a ghost in my house; while I don't entirely believe in that stuff, I've had some weird shit happen to me in the past that has opened my eyes a little. I'm never the first to call anything haunted unless I get hardcore proof. With the weird shit that's been happening, I wouldn't not call it something paranormal.

He chuckled again. "You don't believe in that stuff, do you?" I stood up, and we walked downstairs. "I mean, what just happened was freaky, but I wouldn't peg it as supernatural."

I went to the fridge and grabbed two beers, offering him one that he took. "This house has some weird shit that goes on. You can't look me in the eye and tell me that what you saw in the window wasn't a spirit because it just disappeared. There isn't another living thing in here." He shrugged a bit and took a drink of his beer. "It's not just that or the photos. Now and then, I'll find things have moved on their own, my tools will be on the other side of the room, or I'll wake up and my TV will be turned on. At first, I just chalked it up to me being exhausted from working so much, but after it kept happening, I knew it wasn't me." I took a long drink. "I can also hear things at night; again, at first, I just thought it was the house settling, but some of the noises are too distinct. Sometimes it sounds like footsteps, and sometimes, it sounds like someone's hitting the walls. And every night, it sounds like someone is rocking on a really old rocking chair in the attic."

Teddy looked at me as if he was studying me and

trying to figure out what to say. I know I probably sound crazy to someone who doesn't believe it, but it's a little freaky, right? Eventually, he nodded, "Okay, let's take a look."

I quirked an eyebrow. "What?"

"Let's go up to the attic. I'm sure what you're hearing is old wood settling as you do your renovations." He set his beer on the counter, and I did the same with a sigh. "And I'm telling you, all these houses just have beams for attics; you can barely even use them for storage." I lead him upstairs to the hatch door in the ceiling. It was about three feet long and had a small loop at the end to pull it down. I opened the hall closet and pulled out the hook needed to pull down the door.

Teddy took the hook, and I stood out of the way so he could pull it down. As he did, I jumped slightly at the loud thudding of the ladder as it swung down with the door. I shared a look with Teddy, and he looked a bit confused. "Didn't you say the other houses were built later? My guess is they weren't built the same either." We looked up at the opening to the attic. There was a hint of light, but not enough to see clearly.

Teddy took the initiative and started up the ladder, I followed close behind, and as soon as we were both up, we turned on the flashlights on our phones to see better. The small light was coming from a tiny window in the center point of the ceiling. The attic was more finished than expected, the walls were still open beams, but the wooden floor was complete. It was extremely dusty, and I'm sure there were a ton of spiders hiding around here.

It was empty; I couldn't see anything up there with the light we had. It made me feel a little bit better, but not much. I'm sure Teddy only wanted to come up here to make me feel stupid for even thinking I had a ghost. Once I was tired of looking at the empty room, I was ready to go back downstairs. I turned around to find Teddy looking at something. His body was blocking whatever his light was on, so I went to stand closer and looked over his shoulder.

I couldn't hold back the gasp or the crazy shiver that ran down my spine. In the far corner of the attic, so far back you wouldn't be able to see it until you put a light on it, was an antique rocking chair. The old wood was dark brown and had intricate carvings over it. There was an inscription on the top, so I stepped closer to read it. "Oscar and Mildred Smith: January 11th, 1952" was carved with swirling letters and little hearts around it. I guess it was a wedding present, given the inscription date.

I looked over the chair more, and more shivers ran through me as I noticed that the dust had been moved on the arms and where the legs would rock down. The chair had been moved; I didn't imagine the pattern of the noises. I looked back at Teddy, who hadn't moved, but he looked very pale. "Believe me now?" He stayed quiet, but I could see the slight nod. I couldn't help the little smirk, feeling better about the fact that I was right. "Let's go." I moved him back to the ladder, and he headed down first. I took one last look at the rocking chair before leaving and closing the door.

Teddy took a huge swig of his beer when we returned to the kitchen. "I mean, that still doesn't really prove that the place is haunted, you know." He spoke after a moment, but he didn't even sound like he believed it. "What are you gonna do?"

I shrugged. "I'm not leaving, I love this house too much, and I've put in too much work. If he's trying to scare me off, it's not gonna work." I looked around as I spoke as if I was trying to direct it at someone else.

"Maybe if you get rid of the rocking chair, it'll make it go away." He offered, and I shrugged. I wasn't quite sure how I felt about it. The only thing that it's done that was extra creepy was take pictures of me, which I still don't understand why. There hasn't been anything really menacing that has been going on, but who's to say that won't change?

"I'll think about it," I said, ending the topic. After the beer was finished, Teddy went home, and I was left alone again. I looked around and sat on the couch in silence, the only noise coming from the kids outside.

I sighed and kind of felt stupid for it, but I started to speak. "If there is someone here – if it's the previous owners or whoever – I'm not here to hurt you or the house. I love this house, and I want to make it better and fix it up so that it doesn't end up breaking down. I know that it might upset you that I'm changing it, but I want to improve it. And you may not like me being here, but this is my home now. You're not going to scare me away; you can take my picture and move things, it doesn't matter; I'm not scared. But I'm okay with coexisting if you can settle down a bit. I'll bring the rocking chair down so you don't have to sit in that cramped corner. But if you do anything worse, I will get rid of it, and I know you probably don't want that." I paused and listened, trying to see if there was any sign of an answer. "I am willing to live peacefully with you here as long as you can do the same. If you agree, can you give me a sign?"

It was silent for a while, almost too long; I thought either I was just crazy for speaking to the empty air or whoever was here didn't want to give up his house. I sighed and rubbed my eyes, trying to figure out how I would deal with an angry ghost, but then I heard a sound. It was quiet, but I could hear the distinct sound of the rocking chair in the attic. It made me smile. "I guess we have a deal."

It's been three months since that day, and most of the renovations are done; I'm still working on a few more things, but nothing as extreme as gutting the kitchen and bathroom. I cleaned up the lawn and fence and power washed and painted it so it looked new again. My mom and sister came over at some point to give it the "feminine touch" by planting a garden out front. The backyard was also de-weeded and fixed up. I plan on rebuilding the deck at some point, but it probably won't be until spring. The house is looking a lot homier.

Of course, when she came over, my mom did mention the old rocking chair. I told her I found it in the attic and liked it, so I brought it down to the living room. I didn't feel the need to tell her the whole story and scare her. Though, since bringing it down, the activity has become almost non-existent. There aren't any more weird pictures on my phone, thank god. I found a box behind the rocking chair filled with photobooks of Oscar and Mildred, the previous owners. They took an abundance of pictures like they never wanted to forget anything they did. My guess is that my photo was taken because it was a way he knew how to communicate. I still don't really understand it, but that was the best explanation I could come up with. Every so often, I still find something moved, but it's mostly a picture frame slid across a shelf or a cup sitting on the counter, even if it was in the cupboard.

The one thing that has stayed constant is the nightly creaking of the rocking chair. At this point, I've gotten used to the sounds, and since they're down in the living room and not right over my head, they aren't as loud. It's become a bit of a comforting sound, to be honest. We kept our promise to each other, and we got to live happily in the house.

www.ingramcontent.com/pod-product-compliance
Lightning Source LLC
Chambersburg PA
CBHW060926140726
47996CB00001B/394